Milwaukee's Revenge

Ryan Alexander

Primedia E-launch LLC

ISBN: 978-1-64871-766-6 (Paperback)
ISBN: 978-1-64871-774-1 (EBook)

Any references to historical events, real people, or real places are used
fictitiously. Names, characters, and places are products of the author's
imagination.

Front cover image by Kaitlyn Alexander.

First printing edition 2020.

Primedia E-launch LLC
14575 N. Luckett Rd
Marana, AZ 85653

www.facebook.com/ryan.alexander.90

To my Papaw, George "Doc" Alexander, thank you for showing me that all things are possible.

Contents

Milwaukee's Revenge

Part 1

Chapter 1

2014

Brian

The Night of June 5th

We were shuffling through the doors of Miller Stadium like seniors on the last day of school. Hannah was holding my hand, leading the way. She was easy to follow with her blue and yellow ribbon wrapped in her blonde hair. Her hair hung halfway between her shoulders and the middle of her back. She had curled it tonight, and the ribbons looked more like blue and yellow extensions than they did ribbons.

"Go Brewers!" a drunken man called out to no one in particular.

Wisconsin is known for drinking, and if you ever want to see if that fact is true, just go to a sports game. The Packers, Badgers, and Brewers are all built in reasons for people to drink. What made this night even more of an occasion was that the Brewers actually won. We don't win that often, but when we do, we celebrate.

"Hurry, babe!" Hannah called back to me. She had that slightly buzzed and playful look about her tonight.

I rushed up and picked her about a foot off the ground. As I did, her blue Brewer's shirt slipped up above her hips. I carried her for a few feet and set her down as the crowd came to a standstill. Hannah looked over her shoulder and smiled at me. Even after five years of marriage, her blue eyes still stunned me. She gave me a little kiss as the crowd in front of us inched forward.

"You're a cutie, you know that?" She said with a big smile. "I think I'll keep you."

My arms were still around her waist when I leaned in and pecked her neck. It wasn't a big make out; it was the kind of drunk, fun, actually love someone kiss. We came to another stop. I pulled her close and whispered, "I think I'll do more than keep you tonight," I laughed as I pecked her ear.

This made Hannah laugh out loud. She turned slightly and looked me in the face.

"Did you say ice cream? Yep. You can get me ice cream tonight," She said laughing.

My wife has a way of changing the subject before I get dirty. Little things like that are why I love her so much. We have created our own little dialogue that every couple does, and this one was ours.

As we got to the parking lot, there were coolers everywhere. People will come to Brewers games and tailgate the whole time. That's liking to drink: go to a baseball game and never leave the parking lot.

We left the stadium in our blue, dually truck and headed towards home. We lived outside the small town of Omro, a little over an hour away from Milwaukee. Hannah was a teacher at a small elementary school. I ran the family farm where we had about two hundred cows. I was a little too buzzed, so Hannah was behind the wheel.

"I think we should get some diesel before we leave the city," she said looking down at the gauge.

"Diesel and an ice cream bar?" I replied, and we both smiled at each other.

"You know me too well, Babe," she said.

Just before we were going to get on Interstate 41 and head north, Hannah pulled into a Kwik Stop. It wasn't the best part of town, but with the Black Lives Matter riots occurring, the streets were empty. I jumped out and pumped the fuel, and once it was done, we headed in for our ice cream bar. Tonight was the kind of night that a person looks back on for many years. We rarely went in to watch games, and we had a great time. We had eaten hot dogs, drank a few beers, and made friends with everyone around us.

Hannah and I walked out of the gas station with our bag of ice cream bars and not a care in the world. We were as light as the cool summer air. It was about 9:30pm and finally dark. The parking lot was fairly lit up, and in the city, a person could still see well. The sun had just gone down.

There was a black kid, around fifteen or so, standing close to our truck looking around nervously. He had on a Chicago Bears, Brian Urlacher jersey that was too big for him.

Just then, we were approached by two black men and a black woman. The man on the far left was big and strong. He had a sleeveless blue shirt on and arms that would make you want to go sleeveless. He had tattoos on his arms, but I couldn't make out what they were, just that they were there. He had cornrows in his hair and a square jaw.

"Ain't you a pretty bitch?" the woman in the middle said to Hannah as they were approaching. This woman was the definition of a Ho. She had a low cut white shirt on that said "PINK" across it. She had apparently cut the shirt to make it even more low cut because now it said "P then there were two big pushed up boobs followed by a K". She had tight, ripped, blue jeans on and some kind of heeled shoes. They weren't stilettos, just something that made her an inch taller. Her makeup was thick, and there was not a glimpse of class to be seen.

"Excuse me," Hannah answered bewildered.

"You heard me, Bitch," the woman replied.

Hannah started to bow up out of instinct, and I said, "Hey," But I was cut off by the third man.

"Shut the fuck up," he said, and I could tell that there was going to be a fight by his tone. This man was shorter than me and was wearing an untucked blue and white button up shirt with long sleeves. He was wearing a Milwaukee Bucks hat with a flat brim and the sticker still on the bill.

"You white motherfuckers think you can come around here and talk to us like nothing," he said.

Hannah and I kept walking toward the truck, now taking quicker steps. We were holding hands, and she was slightly pulling me along. Hannah doesn't like confrontation and was trying to get out of Dodge before stuff really hit the fan.

"Get 'em," the third man yelled to the others as they started after us.

There was no way we would make it to the truck, so I turned and was ready to fight. I'm not a fighter, but when you're backed into a corner, you either fight or flee, and tonight I wasn't going to flee.

"Call the cops!" I hollered to Hannah as I flung the bag of ice cream at the oncoming group.

The bag flew and hit the shorter man in the face. It didn't cause any damage, probably just pissed him off more. Once I was fully turned, they hesitated for just a second, and then I felt a fist hit me in the back of the head. Someone grabbed a hold of me from behind and was trying to push me to the ground. He had gotten slightly off balance and was not directly behind me. He was over my left shoulder, and I elbowed him directly in the face. I'm talking an elbow that would have made an onlooker flinch.

When I looked over my shoulder, I couldn't believe it. The man was white. He was a skinny tweeker looking man in a prototypical wife beater shirt. I turned back toward the three but was too late. The big one hit me in the face, and the shorter man started hitting me in the back of the head and neck until I was on the ground face down. Then I could feel feet kicking me in the sides. I looked up and the Ho was even kicking me. I felt like a steak in the middle of a pack of dogs.

"That's right, Motherfucker. Eat it. Eat it!" the shorter man was yelling.

I was basically in the fetal position getting the shit kicked out of me when I saw the white guy again. He had blood down the front of his wife beater and a knife in his hand. It was just a little switchblade, but it was still a knife.

The crowd stopped kicking me and slightly opened up for Mr. Whitetrash. I knew he was going to stab me. There wasn't much I could do but hope that someone would pull up. I was having a hard enough time breathing, let alone trying to fight back. He grabbed me by the shirt, and as he was about to stick me, my wish was granted. Only my

5

wish was granted by the one person I wish wouldn't have stepped forward, Hannah. She was screaming and pushed the man off of me.

That was the biggest mistake she could have made. It would have been better to let the man cut me from ear to ear. The shorter man grabbed Hannah and punched her square in the face. Hannah stumbled but didn't go completely down. He then grabbed her head and pushed it toward the ground. She was too close to the cement separating the fuel pumps, so she hit the back of her head and didn't move. That hurt me more than any of their blows could have ever done.

"No!" I yelled, but the big man got on top of me and began hitting me in the face repeatedly.

Everything was blurry and ringing in my head. I could hear someone else screaming, but it sounded like it was coming from every direction. I could feel my neck pop with each hit. The man finally got off me and was pulling my wallet out my front pocket. I rolled and could see Hannah lying motionless.

"I'm getting mine," I heard somebody yell. The whitetrash man leaned down and stabbed Hannah in the left side of her stomach. He did it quickly, and I couldn't move to help. I wanted to yell. My mouth would open, but no sound was coming out. I could feel blood running down my nose. He turned and with a jump in my direction, was kneeling by me now. I felt a sharp pain in my right side, just below my ribs. I knew I had been stabbed, but it didn't hurt as badly as I was expecting. The man then spit in my face. The only thing I could do was close my eyes.

"Don't ever come here again, or I'll kill you, Motherfucker," a voice said.

I opened my eyes to see the short black man looking me in the face.

"Black Lives Matter. Bitch Lives Don't."

He stood up and started to jog away. He grabbed his woman's arm as he went by her. She kicked Hannah in the stomach as they headed towards a car.

"Black Lives Matter, Motherfucker!" The woman yelled out with two middle fingers in the air. She was laughing like Harley Quinn.

The shorter black man got in the passenger seat of the white car. When the door was open, I could see the black kid in the Urlacher jersey in the driver's seat. The big black man, black woman, and Mr. Whitetrash got in the back. Once they were all in, the car sped away.

I started to crawl toward Hannah. She still wasn't moving. My head was pounding, and everything was fading in and out. There were black spots everywhere I looked. I was still crawling toward her when everything went black. The last thought I had was "Why us?" We were both motionless as the blue and red lights came into sight.

Chapter 2

Detective Jack Owens

The Night of June 5th

The ambulance pulled out just as we were pulling into the parking lot. My partner and I got the call but were on the other side of Miller Stadium at the time. We weren't that far from the Kwik Stop, but with the traffic leaving the game, it had taken twice as long to get there.

"What's up?" I asked the officer walking towards us.

Chuck was an older officer, slightly overweight with unusually long gray side burns. He had been a cop over twenty years and had seen just about everything there was to see in Milwaukee.

"See that woman over there?" Chuck said pointing at a Hispanic woman who looked to be in her early forties. "She walked up on a young couple being beaten and robbed. She didn't get a good look at who did it because she was calling the cops, only that there was a couple black guys, maybe a couple of white guys, and a couple of women."

"Damn, you're saying that two people got beat up by a mixed group of six?" Eddie, my partner, asked confused.

"No, the people who got the shit knocked out of them were the white ones. The black ones were the ones that assaulted them," Chuck clarified.

"How is the couple doing?" I asked

"Not good. They tuned the husband up pretty good, and the wife cracked her head open. Most of the blood over there is from her." He pointed to where the couple had been laying, and there was a decent amount of blood on the ground.

"Any ideas on a motive? Robbery or just the fun of beating a young couple up?" I asked.

"Yeah, how about a hate crime. The woman, Ms. Martinez, said she heard the black girl yell 'Black Lives Matter' as they left," Chuck said.

My partner and I looked at each other. This is not what we needed right now, and we both knew it. Just four days before an officer on our force, Jason Newton, a good friend of mine, shot and killed a young black kid in Milwaukee. Officer Newton had done nothing wrong. At a routine stop, this black kid got out of his Honda Civic and pointed a gun at Newton's partner. Newton drew his weapon and told him to get on the ground. That's when the law abiding citizen then pointed his gun at Newton who shot the now famous Lamar Webb.

Of course, Lamar was a five star football recruit signed and sealed to play in the SEC. The national news got a hold of the story, and before the facts were even released, Officer Jason Newton was, in one word, fucked. Everyone came forward talking about how good of a young man Lamar was and how "He would never do anything wrong." There were pictures of him holding babies and shaking hands with the mayor after they won the state championship last year.

Even that son of a bitch mayor was pouring it on Officer Newton by taking the kid's side. He got on CNN and said, "I personally knew Lamar, and he was a great young man. These racist acts have to stop."

Prick. Not a good word was said about Jason Newton, a man he actually did know. This story wouldn't be complete without irony, and we had more irony to pass around than blame.

The first bit of irony is that this "racist" act was committed by Officer Jason Newton, a black man. Not a Russell Wilson kind of black man either. Jason was born on the south side of Chicago and had three brothers gunned down before he graduated high school. He worked himself through the police academy and was now one of the most liked cops on the force. He became a cop because one had helped him make it out of Chicago, and he was going to pass it forward to as many kids he could.

The second bit of irony had started occurring after one night of the national news. The Black Lives Matter movement had been in full force every night in Milwaukee for the past three nights. Just as I'm sure Martin Luther King Jr. would have wanted, every night was filled with riots and looting. Black lives matter, but I guess black stores don't. Over half of the stores being looted were owned or run by black men. There had been one additional death because of the riots.

This leads us to our final piece of irony. The man who was killed at the riot was a cop trying to calm the crowd down. He did not have his weapon drawn when a rioter, a black man, walked up and shot him in the head. The officer was named Jeffery Jackson, and to complete the irony circle, yes, he too was a black man.

A little recap: A black kid was shot by a black cop, so a black group of protestors looted black owned stores, and a black rioter then shot a black cop. All the while, the white newscasters on every news channel around the country told their white viewers that "racism" is destroying our country.

Which brings us back to why our current situation was the absolute worse time for this crime to occur. Milwaukee was a fire waiting to explode, and we didn't need to throw gasoline on it just to watch the flames rise.

"Eddie, why don't you get Ms. Martinez's statement, and I'll take a look at this blood scene. We need to get to the hospital and get that young couple's statement before this thing gets out of control," I told my partner as we nodded at each other and separated.

"You know this whole thing looks bad, right?" Chuck asked me once I was alone.

"I know," I said low enough that only he could hear.

"If that young couple happens to die, a lot of people will want blood. If you bust these black folks, even if they're guilty, that group rioting ten minutes from here will be surrounding the station. Better do shit right, Detective," he said.

I took a deep breath and nodded at Chuck. He had been around, and he was right. Earlier that night, I was eating a ham sandwich from Subway and thinking that things had to start slowing down. Boy, had I been wrong.

Chapter 3

Brian

The Morning of June 6th

The light blinded me as I tried to pry my eyes open. So far, my right eye was the only one able let any light in. My left eye felt like it got replaced with a baseball, and I couldn't open it. I heard a constant beeping, and I couldn't tell if it was in my head or coming from around me. For a brief second, I was so disconnected that I thought I might be dead, but that was interrupted quickly by the sight of human life.

A nurse walked in and smiled when she saw that I was awake. She looked like a cafeteria lady who was smart enough to stay in school but was most likely still single because she was "in love with her work." She had a clip board in her hand and looked down at it before she spoke.

"Mr. Walker, how do you feel?" She asked

I tried to open my mouth, but my jaw felt like it had a crack in it. It felt like if I tried to force it open, it might pop.

"That's ok; you don't have to move, Mr. Walker. Just try to get some rest," she said casually while checking my beeping machine. She turned to walk out the room when I mustered out a word.

"Hannah," I pushed out through the pain.

The nurse turned over her shoulder and looked at me. Her look lacked hope and displayed sadness. She forced a smile.

"You just get some rest, Mr. Walker. We're doing everything we can for your wife," she said and walked out of my room.

This comment was unsettling. My heart started to race. I could tell because my beeping machine was lighting up faster than it was before. The thought of Hannah lying somewhere else in the hospital made fear wrap its filthy hands around me. If she was doing well, the nurse would have led with that news.

Chapter 4

Detective Owens

The Morning of June 6th

I hate hospitals. I avoid them like the plague, partially because they might actually be filled with a plague. Sitting in the waiting room may be the worse part of all. I was surrounded by sick kids having a game of who could touch the cleanest thing before the other one. A woman was three chairs down and was randomly dry heaving every few minutes. If she didn't stop, I was going to throw up.

My partner, Eddie Thompson, left me here while he ventured to the hallway to talk on the phone. He said it was for the case, but he must have forgotten I'm a detective. He's about 6'1 and very skinny. He has thin brown hair that was always too long on top but cut short on the sides. Eddie had a pointy nose and looked more like he should be on his way to poetry reading than a cop. He covers this up by generally being a dick all the time. But when he's on the phone with his girlfriend, he looks like his favorite poet just wrote about whip-poor-wills and bunny rabbits.

Finally, the doctor walked up and waved me over to him. I gave Eddie the "get off the phone" look, and we all headed towards the doctor's office. Dr. Raj Shapour was the Walkers' attending. He looked just like the doctors on TV, blue scrubs with a white coat over it. To top it off, he had a stethoscope around his neck. Once we were in his office and got through the introductions, I began the questions.

"How is Mr. Walker doing?" I asked.

"The nurse just reported to me that he is awake but barely able to communicate," he said.

"Would we be able to ask him a few questions?"

"Detective, last night he sustained cracked ribs, a collapsed lung, multiple facial fractures, not to mention a stab wound. He was unconscious for hours and still probably can't speak in full sentences. I doubt you'll get much out of him," the doctor said.

"How about Mrs. Walker?"

"She's the one we're really worried about. She has an intracranial hemorrhage and has been unconscious the whole time," he said.

"I'm sorry Doc, but what does that mean?" I asked.

"Basically, that means that her brain is swelling and has yet to stop. If it doesn't stop soon, and I mean very soon, we're gonna have a big problem," he said looking serious between the two of us. "Are there any suspects yet?"

Just as I was about to speak, Eddie butted in and spoke which was rare.

"Uh, no, no suspects yet," he said making sure I couldn't answer.

I glanced over my shoulder and looked at Eddie. As he met my gaze, Eddie raised his chin towards me and focused on the doctor. This little act of defiance was the first one in our fourteen month partnership. I am only thirty two years old and still look like I'm twenty five. Eddie is twenty nine and looks like he is in college. In our time together, we have never jumped on each other's sentences or done anything to make people think less of us. We already had a disadvantage because people looked at us like we were too young. Nobody wants to get interviewed by two guys who look more like Mormon missionaries than school detectives.

"Thank you, Doctor. We'll give Mr. Walker a little more time before we ask him any questions," I said and shook the doctor's hand.

As we walked down the hallway, Eddie and I didn't speak. I was trying to figure out what his angle was on this. It wasn't that he said something terribly wrong, it was the way he said it and how abnormal it was for him. Three nurses got off the elevator, and it was open as we stepped in and pressed M.

As the doors closed, Eddie was quick to speak.

"Hey, man, I'm sorry for stepping on you back there," he said and seemed sincere. "Captain called me and didn't want any details told to anyone."

"Why didn't he tell me that?" I asked

"I don't know, man. He just sternly told me to not let any details out until he could talk to me in person. I wasn't even supposed to tell you, but I don't want any rifts between us. So if Captain asks, you didn't hear this shit from me," Eddie said.

I just nodded my head. I truly didn't understand why Captain would say that and especially why he wouldn't want me to know.

"I'm serious, man, not a word. If he does tell you, you better act like it's all new to you too. I don't want my ass chewed for trying to be a good partner," he said.

"I gotchya, bud. Not a word," I said.

The doors opened up on the second floor, and an old man stepped on. He had been crying and had a solemn look on his face. He didn't even know anyone else was on the elevator. My guess would be that he either received bad news or maybe even the worst news. We stopped talking and waited to get off on the main floor.

As we left the hospital, all I could think of was why I had been left out by the Captain. Maybe he was just trying to give Eddie some more responsibility. Maybe I did something to piss him off. Or maybe there was something fishy going on. Eddie would be a lot easier for the Captain to influence than I would be. I'm not Mr. Backbone by any stretch, but Eddie was a go along guy. If you were going to a party or to church, he'd go along if everyone else was going. He was at the stage of his career where if the Captain asked him to jump, he would have jumped in front of traffic if it would have gotten him noticed.

Sometimes I have conspiracy theories, and this was probably one of them. The Captain would probably tell me as soon as we got there and this would have been for nothing. We just needed one of the Walkers to get to a point so that we could ask them some questions. Time was already not on our side, and we needed to get moving on this. Call it intuition or just getting used to being a detective, but something just didn't feel right about the whole situation.

Chapter 5

Detective Owens

Afternoon of June 6th

Eddie got the call, and now we were waiting to go into the Captain's office. Eddie got the call, not me. I kept telling myself that everything was fine, but I had a sour feeling in my gut. Sitting in front of the Captain's office feels a lot like waiting to be seen by the Principal. You are either about to get a pat on the back or an ear full. Everyone knows it, and those who walk by secretly hope it's the ear full.

Finally, the door opened, and the Captain waved us in. Captain James Stroup was in his early fifties and very overweight. He was completely bald; he started out with the Homer Simpson hairdo, but in the past few years had bicked the rest of it off. The older officers say that he wasn't always heavy, but his promotion was followed by a divorce, and the pieces were put together with pizza and glaze.

"Sit down," the Captain said as he closed the door behind us.

As the Captain sat down at his desk, he took his left hand and began to rub his temples with his thumb and middle finger. He was looking down at his desk. His thumb was staying in place while his middle finger was kneading away. Eddie and I looked at each other, but neither one of us was stupid enough to start the conversation.

On the Captain's desk there were two pictures facing the visitors. The one on the left was of his family. This was pre-divorce and was about ten years old. The Captain had a chubby, red headed wife and two chubby, red headed daughters. It was like Raggedy Ann became Midwestern Ann times three.

The other picture was of himself and Aaron Rodgers. The Captain had a big shit eating grin on his face, and Aaron had a little smirk that I'm sure he puts on for all his pictures. The Captain had on his number twelve Packers jersey over his cop uniform. He looked like a combination of a typical Wisconsin man and a douche bag. I chuckled to myself. That picture had caught the perfect description of the Captain.

"These past few days have been hell for us. First, we have the heat coming down for Officer Newton. Now these riots. Every god damn news station wants a sound bite. I'm even supposed to be on *The O'Reilly Factor* tonight." The Captain finally smirked. "The No Fucking Spin Zone. Unbelievable."

Deep down, and by deep down, I mean just below the false surface, both of us knew that the Captain loved the attention. He might not like why he was on *The O'Reilly Factor*, but you can bet this was going to be a conversation starter the rest of his life.

"Now, Boys, I'm going to take this on behalf of the department. Somebody has to take the hit. That's what it means to be team players." He looked from Eddie to me and then back to Eddie. "Are you boys willing to be team players? To put the department before everything?"

"Yes sir," Eddie answered before he stuck his nose completely up the Captain's ass.

I just nodded. When a person tells you how much they've done for the department, and then asks if you're willing to do something for the same department, you can bet the request is going to be more than you'd bargain for.

"Good," the Captain nodded in approval, "Do you men understand why a race fueled case would not be good right now?"

We both nodded. I also took note that before we said we'd do anything for the department, we were "boys", but now we're on his side, so now we're "men." I looked over at Eddie and he was soaking it up. This little "Boys to Men" comment had pissed me off, but he looked more like a fifteen-year-old girl at a "Boyz 2 Men" concert yelling, "pick me."

"I would never ask you not solve a case. That's unethical, and those words would never come out of my mouth." He said this while raising a finger to us in a scolding manner. "But, this case needs to be muffled for a bit."

"Muffled, Sir?" I asked.

"Yes, Owens, muffled. We don't need anyone getting in front of the cameras and screaming that a few blacks did this for no reason. We just need to muffle this until things cool down," he said.

"I understand," Eddie replied.

"How exactly do we muffle this, Sir?" I asked because, unlike Mr. Ass-kisser, I didn't understand.

The Captain did not like my questions but was trying to keep his cool. Unfortunately for him, his bald head was like a temperature gauge that he couldn't hide. As soon as he started to get flustered, his head would start to turn red. This would increase until he was bright red and veins were popping out from the sides. Right now, the oven was on, but he was still at a light pink. He took a deep breath.

"The first thing is you're going to make sure our witness is credible, both in her story and her life. Eddie, I want you to go over and over Ms Martinez's story and find any cracks. If her story is true, there won't be any. If it isn't, then find them."

"Will do, Cap. If there are cracks, I'll find them," Eddie said in his valiant voice.

"Good. Second, I want you to make sure the Walkers' version can hold up in court. If they were too loopy, I don't want to find that out in front of a judge. Maybe, wait a few days to let their minds clear up," he said.

"Captain, I don't know if that's a good…" That was all I got out before being cut off.

"God damn it, Owens, do you wanna be the Captain? Huh, do you wanna trade me seats?" He stood up and his head was red, but the veins weren't showing yet.

"No, Sir," I said like a whipped dog.

"That's right, no fucking sir you don't. It's easy to question on that side of the desk. Do you want another cop dead like at the riot? Do you want that on your head?" He was standing behind his desk staring at me.

"No, Sir," I said again.

"You've got a lot to learn, Owens. Maybe this will be good for you. Thompson, you're taking point on this one. You ask the questions, and Owens backs you up." He was now looking at Eddie. "You bring me a report at the end of every day. Just you. And don't leave anything out.

21

Any evidence you find, I want to see it. I'm not sticking this department's neck out on the line for some bullshit piece of evidence that will never stick. Got it?"

"Yes, sir," we both answered.

"Good," he answered and had to catch his breath. "Now get out there and do some police work."

We left the room without handshakes and walked back towards our desks. I was baffled. I got reprimanded for trying to do the right thing, and Eddie got a mini promotion for being an ass kisser. What the hell was going on? Politics is in every field. It doesn't matter if you're a politician or a factory worker, there's always politics. But for the first time in person, I just saw politics replace justice.

Chapter 6

Brian

The Morning of June 7th

I had never felt more helpless in my whole life. I was sitting with Hannah's hand in mine. The wheel chair that the nurse made me use was awkward, but I maneuvered it as close as I could to her side. She looked peaceful lying there in her bed. She was not conscious and hadn't been since we got to the hospital. There were machines and lights everywhere, and in the chaos, she still looked peaceful.

Hannah's mom was sitting in the corner. She wasn't crying at the moment, but she would be soon. The crying came in spurts. Hannah and her mom, Shelby, are very close. They even look alike. They were both thin blondes with blue eyes. Shelby had the soccer mom haircut, but their similar looks were undeniable. They talked on the phone every other day. Shelby lived in Illinois with her new husband. She couldn't get a flight fast enough, so she drove up here and had been a wreck ever since. I didn't blame her, though. It was shocking to see Hannah with a black eye and half shaven head. No matter how well a person describes someone in a hospital to you, the first glimpse is always painful.

I kept rubbing Hannah's hand with my thumb, thinking her eyes would open. I continually closed my eyes and said little prayers. "Please God, please don't take her. Take me, not her. Please." I repeated this

23

every few minutes but had received no response that said He heard me or that anything was going to change. Every time my thumb bumped into her IV, it was a little reminder that everything was one hundred percent out of my hands. Either God or a doctor would fix her, not me. All I could hope was that one of them did something fast.

The door opened, and the doctor along with three other nurses walked in. The doctor was from a different country, probably India, but seemed very capable. His name was Dr. Shapour, and he gave me a nod as they entered the room.

"It's time?" I asked.

"Yes, Mr. Walker. If you will please go back to your room, I will bring you an update as soon as we are through."

"Kelly, will you please see Mr. Walker back to his room?" He asked one of the nurses.

She was the same nurse who wheeled me over the first time. She was about my age with brunette hair and was probably pregnant. I couldn't guarantee it, but I'd bet a lot on it. She had the pregnant stance. She put her fist on her side angling toward her back. When she did, she straightened up and took a semi deep breath. She cried every time she came into Hannah's room.

"Are you ready, Mr. Walker?" She asked, already holding back the tears.

I did not approve or disapprove as she began to roll me away. I just stared at Hannah, hoping to see her with her eyes open again. The other two nurses were getting Hannah's bed ready to roll to surgery. I knew I couldn't stay, but I didn't want to go. I was what I had been for a day now, helpless.

Dr. Shapour had gone through what her surgery was going to entail in my room. Hannah's brain had not quit swelling, so they were going to cut out a piece of her skull and surgically place it in her side. This way, her brain could swell while causing less damage, and they put it in her side in hopes that it will keep better until they put it back. I signed a paper, and she was going under the knife this morning.

As the nurse was wheeling me back, a toddler went running and screaming down the hall. He wasn't wearing a gown, so I guessed one of his parents or siblings was the patient in the hospital. Kelly stopped the wheel chair and locked it into place.

"Hold on, one second, Mr. Walker," she said as she started after the escapee.

To my right, there was a silver push cart that had been freshly cleaned. The side showed a perfect reflection. I hadn't seen a mirror since we'd arrived in the hospital. I looked at myself and couldn't believe it. My face was perfectly round from all the swelling. I knew that my eyes were swollen because I could still barely open the left one. But the image didn't even look like me. Below my eyes but above my jaw was mostly a combination of black, blue, and purple.

I tried to turn the wheels away from the cart so I wouldn't have to look at it. The damn wheels were locked into place, and I couldn't get them to budge. I could hear them wheeling Hannah's bed in the other direction behind me. I sat back in my chair and closed my eyes. "Please God, let Hannah come out of this. Please," I prayed silently. When I opened my eyes, I was still looking at the cart. Only now, there were tears coming down my face. The only thing worse than being helpless is knowing that you're helpless.

Chapter 7

Detective Owens

The Afternoon of June 7th

That was painful. I just witnessed a law abiding, Good Samaritan citizen get annihilated in an interrogation room for nearly two hours. Eddie was my partner but right now he was a piece of shit in my book. Ms. Martinez came to the station wanting to help and now probably wouldn't piss on us if we were on fire.

Sabrina Martinez showed up to the station in a beautiful white sun dress with big yellow and orange flowers around her hips. She had even done her hair. At one time, she had been an attractive woman. Time and most likely a hard life lined her otherwise pretty face. She still had a glow about her as she walked in the conference room. She didn't look like she was going on a date, more like she was meeting a friend for brunch.

It started with pleasantries, and we assured her that she didn't need a lawyer. Of course, she never suspected that she would need one since she didn't do anything wrong. Her story was quite simple when she arrived. She knew that the Walkers got attacked by a few black people. One of them was a woman, and they drove away in a white car. Before they left, the woman yelled out "Black Lives Matter." By the end of her frustrating session, she now *thought* there could have been a few black people, one of them *might* have been a woman but wasn't sure, and it *looked like* a white car but she could not tell the model, so she wasn't really sure about the vehicle. She thought she heard someone yell out "Black lives Matter," but that could have been an echo from the riots.

Anger was smeared across her face. Eddie had treated her like an imbecile who didn't know left from right. When people speak, they often say words like "um", "ya", and "I think" without ever knowing they said them. Eddie would use these meaningless words against her. The art is in asking specific questions that she didn't know and then expanding that to affect what she thought she did know. An example would be:

"Was the car a Ford?"

"I don't know."

"Was it a Chevy?"

"I don't know."

"Was it Toyota?"

"I don't know."

"Was it white or off white?"

"I think white."

"Could it have been dirty so you couldn't tell?"

"Yeah, I guess it could have been."

"So basically, you don't know what kind of car it was but you think could have been white."

"Yeah."

Ms. Martinez was positive it was a white car when she walked in but now was on record that she "thinks it could have been white." After nearly two hours of this, a person isn't sure what they saw, and even if they were sure, their account would never hold up in court.

I never said a word the entire interview. Occasionally, Ms. Martinez would look at me for help, and like a shitty parent, I'd just look the other way. She even asked us several times if she needed a lawyer. Like a crappy cop show, Eddie would reply, "You're not on trial, Ms. Martinez" or the classic "Only guilty people need a lawyer," and we'd tread on.

Ms. Martinez left with no goodbye and no way in hell she'd help us again. Sometimes I can't imagine why cops have a bad name, but on days like this, I completely understand. Eddie had an agenda and accomplished it. I watched her walk down the hall with her head held high. She may been disrespected, but she still had her pride.

"Well, I'd consider her muffled." Eddie smiled like a little kid who got an A on his spelling test. "Let's go write this up."

I stood in the doorway for a second. It is amazing how primal we humans really are. Alphas will always bully Betas whether we are in grade school or cops at the station. If a person has power, they can't help but exercise it over the weak. Ms. Martinez was just bullied. Eddie received a little power and couldn't help but wield it. I just couldn't figure out which side I was on. Was I on the receiving end of having power wielded by Captain Stroup, or did I just enable Eddie to use his power over Ms. Martinez? I know there is a heaven and a hell; it's the devil that lingers in the middle.

Chapter 8

Brian

The Morning of June 8th

Every breath in felt like the end of a knife was being sharply driven into my side. The deeper I would breathe in, the deeper the knife would go. It was a constant reminder of that night. Last night, my face was starting to lose some of the swelling. There was a glimmer of hope beginning to set in for the first time since being in the hospital. Hannah's surgery was successful, and my face was finally beginning the long road to recovery. During my final prayer of the night, I even felt what I thought was peace.

Life woke me up with nothing short of a big "fuck you." The pain was so sharp with my first morning breath that I gasped. This only caused my second morning breath to be even more painful. I went from lying down to sitting up with my toes pointing. The damn nurse clicker was nowhere to found.

"Nurse… Nurse!" I called hoping someone would come in.

A male nurse walked through my door, and when he saw me holding me side, he hurried over to me.

"Sir, are you ok? What happened?" He asked.

"It's my side when I breathe," I said wincing.

"Ok sir, I'm going to run and get Kelly. She's just a few doors down. Just try to stay calm," he said and walked quickly left the room.

I had never liked the thought of male nurses, but this son of a bitch just spoiled it for the rest of them. I felt like my side was under attack, and he just left me hanging there alone. If I got through this, I might have to go ape shit on Mr. Metro.

Kelly came rushing into my room. She had on pink scrubs and her hair in a ponytail.

"Mr. Walker, are you ok?" She asked.

"It's my side when I breathe," I said for the second time in under a minute. Amazingly, it didn't hurt as badly this time as it did with the male nurse.

Kelly looked at my side and back at my face. I could almost see the relief pass over her like a single breeze floating through the room.

"Mr. Walker, it's your cracked ribs," she said with sympathy.

"They haven't hurt like this yet," I replied.

"That's pretty normal. At first, your face hurt the worst, but it will also heal the quickest. Now your ribs are gonna hurt the worst, only they're gonna hurt for awhile now," she said

I tried to force a smile and ended up with only a nod. Slowly, I laid back down on my bed. I was forced to submit to the inevitable. Kelly was in full pregnancy stance now as she relaxed from her jog down the hallway.

"Any update on Hannah?" I asked, knowing that there likely wasn't yet.

Kelly smiled and within seconds was blinking to keep the tears away. She shook her head.

"Nothing new yet." She grabbed my hand nearest her. "But she's fighting, and that's good, Mr. Walker."

I nodded my head and squeezed her hand. Kelly was very warm, not to the touch, but in her heart. I thought she truly wanted the best for Hannah and me. She left before any tears fell this time.

So there I was, alone with every breath jabbing me. Life was truly kicking me while I was down. I'd laugh if it didn't hurt so much. Last night, I thought things were turning around. Now, I was in more pain than ever. With each passing hour, the weight of Hannah's unconsciousness weighed heavier on me. Doubt had slithered its way into my mind. Would she ever wake up?

Chapter 9

Detective Owens

The Morning of June 8th

I went into work this morning hoping that today would be a better day. I showed up a little early, so I waited in my truck for a few minutes. I drive a half ton, extended cab, black Dodge. It's not a big truck, but it gets me out of the snow in the winter. I sat there with the morning sports talk radio show on, but I wasn't listening. I spent most of the night debating how big of a piece of shit I really was. So far, the jury was still out. I took a deep breath, and as I exhaled, like Tony Robbins, I told myself to be positive.

The office was quiet in the morning. It was mostly cops sipping on their morning coffee, trying to get the day moving. There was always at least one box of donuts strategically placed in the break room. This might have started as a joke, but the joke's on them. Everyone loved knowing that they're going to be there. They give us a built in reason to congregate in the morning. It's like a water cooler on steroids.

There was something different about today. People were whispering more and were slow to acknowledge me. It wasn't that they didn't, but I had to make the first move. I felt like a high school kid that just got dumped, and now people were hesitant to acknowledge me. I might not be the "cool" one that emerged from the former couple.

Finally, Officer Davis gave me a slap on the back as he walked out of the room.

"Stay after 'em, kid," he said.

Officer Davis was an older cop on the force. He was a nice man and mostly kept to himself. I'd gone out for a fish fry with him once or twice in the last year. His gesture gave me the answer that I needed. The whole force knew about Thompson taking over, and if I had to guess, it was either Eddie or the Chief that spread the word. The rumor mill spins fast on the force. Secrets don't make friends, and cops don't keep secrets, especially after a beer. I took my chocolate glazer and headed for my desk.

As I sat down, my phone vibrated. It was a text from Eddie. It said, "Wait at office, I'll be there soon."

So I sat down at my desk and started looking through paperwork that I should have done a week ago. I figured Eddie would be in within the hour. But when I got through my work, Eddie was still nowhere to be found.

Thirty minutes before lunch, Eddie came strolling in with a bag in his hand. He looked like a high school kid who had won the game last night. His strut should have been in slow motion to punctuate the effect. He was giving everyone the nod as he went by and even pounded fists with Officer Coleman, another young officer on the force while never breaking stride. He didn't walk towards our desks but instead straight to the Captain's office. I noticed that he never looked my way one time.

After a few minutes, Eddie came walking out of the Captain's office. He finally looked at me and gave me a little smirk. As he got to our desks, I sat back in my chair and opened my arms up. This was my way of saying, "What the Fuck?"

"Sorry, man. Captain called me last night, and I had to run an errand for him," Eddie said as he took his jacket off.

"What kind of errand?" I asked.

"Can't really say, but It's cool, man. We're good," he said.

I shook my head and couldn't help but smile. This was unreal. Now they had secret errands, and I was left here all morning with pushing papers.

"Errands, huh? What, do you pick up his laundry now?" I asked sarcastically.

"Something like that," he said and rolled his eyes.

I was done with the morning paperwork, but I started shuffling them again anyways. I didn't want to even look at Eddie right now. You can't wipe smug off someone's face, but you can ignore it.

Chapter 10

Detective Owens

The Afternoon of June 8th

After lunch, I needed to pound the pavement. I didn't become a cop to sit behind a desk, but unfortunately, that was a big part of the job. I can only take so much time in the station before I start to pull my hair out. My limit to how much I can take fluctuates, but with all the shit coming down the pike, I was ready to get out and actually be a police officer.

"You ready, Eddie? They don't pay us to just sit around," I said

I know Eddie heard me, but he never looked up from whatever he was working on. He was filling out some kind of form franticly and looked awkward doing it. When a junior high kid doesn't want his neighbor to cheat on his test, he'll use his opposite arm to cover up his paper while he writes with his good hand. It's almost like a hen using its wing to shield its chick, only the test is their baby. Eddie had this look while he was filling out his paperwork.

I grabbed the paper from Eddie's desk and looked at the top. It was an evidence report. The top line said "Big Jimmy's", the name of a tire shop across the street from the Kwik Stop where the Walkers had been attacked.

"What the fuck is this?" I asked loud enough for several other officers to hear.

Eddie stood up and grabbed the paper out of my hand. The paper ripped at the bottom, but he ended up with the majority of it. Eddie looked furious. He was red, and his hair had fallen down around his eyes. He pointed his finger at me but couldn't make himself speak. I couldn't tell if he was going to hit me or scream like a twelve-year-old girl.

He looked around and noticed that just about everyone was looking at us now. He took a long deep breath and forced a smug smile. Then loud enough for everyone to hear, he announced, "Officer Owens, I need to speak with you in the conference room... *NOW.*"

I took a quick look around, and everyone was watching. Even a punk kid who was waiting for an officer was looking at us. I guess I was just lucky he wasn't recording the whole scene on his cell phone. I looked back at Eddie, and for a moment we just stared each other down. What an arrogant little piece of shit. There was nothing to do but go to the conference room like a little kid who's about to be grounded.

The sound of the door closing could have just as easily been a bell ringing because it signaled that the fight was on.

"What the fuck, man?" This was my verbal first punch.

"Cool it, Jack. It's not what you think it is," he said.

"Let me tell you what I think it is. I think the Captain told you to go down to "Big Jimmy's" and look at their surveillance tape. I think that he told you to go without me. And I think you jumped at the opportunity like a little bitch," I said. "How warm am I?"

"Fuck you, Jack. That's your whole problem; you think you're so fucking smart, don't you?" He said.

"Tell me I'm wrong, Eddie," I said.

"You are wrong. I was just getting them as quick as I could and didn't wait for you. That's all," he said.

"Are you really gonna stand there and bullshit me to my face?" I asked.

Eddie started to speak and then closed his mouth and looked at me.

"The only problem was that I saw your little sheet and now you know that I know you're crossing the line," I said as I pointed me finger at him.

"Crossing the line? Are you fucking crazy? I crossed the line getting *evidence*? He replied.

Eddie smirked and forced a laugh. He now had the look of someone who was winning the fight. He just painted me as going overboard, and we both knew it. If we had been fighting, he just stepped back and let me trip over my own feet.

I was still pointing at him but started to put my finger down. I looked to the big window and saw that most of the officers were looking at our room. I knew they couldn't hear us, but I'm sure they could still see through some of the blinds. Everyone loves a little drama. We would be the talk of the force for the next week.

"Before you accuse me of 'crossing the line', you better have your shit straight. When you say that about me, you're saying it about the Captain too," He said. "And I doubt you want to do that."

He was right. It pissed me off, but he was right. Throwing around accusations on gut feelings was probably not the way to go about this. I nodded my head. We just stood there, and the tension eased out of the room. I finally had to say something.

"Sorry, Man." That's all I could muster.

"We're good. Now let me finish that report, and we can go talk to the Walkers together," he said.

"That'll be good; I need to get out of this place. Shit's making me crazy," I said and we both chuckled.

The feeling in the room had changed dramatically. We were fighting seconds ago, and now we were on the same page again. That's the way it is on the force. It's the closest thing to being on a sports team. Teammates fight and then go back to being teammates as soon as it's over.

"Don't worry, Jack. We're going to get these guys; Captain just wants to make sure that we get the right guys," he said.

That's when my red flag went back up. I smiled at him, but my mind was working again. When did I ever try not to get the right guys? The Captain poured up a big glass of Kool-Aid for Eddie, and he drank the last drop.

Eddie was getting ready to open the door, and I casually asked him one last question.

"So, what was on the tape?"

Eddie held the door handle for a second and then opened it. He turned back to me and smiled for the audience to see.

"Nothing that we'll use," he said and headed to his desk.

Eddie looked like a poet, and sometimes he was crafty with his words.

Chapter 11

Brian

The evening of June 8th

Everyone kept telling me to stay positive. "Stay positive, Mr. Walker," a nurse would say. "Stay positive, Brian," my mother-in-law would say while holding back tears. "Stay positive, my son; God hears our prayers," the priest told me at lunch. I know they're right, but I can't make myself be positive right now. I was in the worst mood of my life.

Why was all of this shit happening to us? We were pretty good people. Hannah and I weren't perfect, but we were above average. If you took me out of the equation, she was a great person. She was a freaking elementary school teacher, for God's sake. Everyone in our little town loved Hannah, and they should. She would go out of her way to help people all the time. Not the way I did it either. I did it when it was convenient or when I would get something out of it. She did it quite literally out of the goodness of her heart. Now, she had been lying in a bed for three days and was still unresponsive.

I had been replaying that night in my head and could remember almost everything. I could even see their faces. There was the short one with a flat brimmed hat who seemed like the leader that pushed Hannah. He had a face that seemed angry at the world, not for having a bad day, but just because he had been born into it. The woman that looked like a stripper kicked Hannah. She wore too much makeup because she thought she was better than the people who don't wear enough. The buff one had beat the shit out of me, but I don't remember him touching Hannah. His face was younger than his muscular body showed. The kid in the Urlacher jersey had driven the white car. He looked like a high school kid who made the wrong choice in his first semester. They had all been black. The tweeker was the only white man and had stabbed us both. He had acne and the face of a junkie looking for his next hit.

I squeezed my fists so hard together that my machine started to beep differently at me. I clenched my teeth and shut my eyes. I wanted to kill them. I wanted revenge for what they had done to Hannah. I might have deserved a beating for something I'd done in life, but she was innocent. She didn't deserve to have these things done to her; they did. If God is a just God, then why was she lying here while they still roamed the streets?

Just then, there was a knock on my door. I looked over and saw that two men were standing in the doorway. I didn't recognize either one, but they were in cheap suits. The one in front had a Johnny Depp haircut and looked like he could be a salesman. The other one looked like he could have been a Marine.

"Come in," I said.

"Thanks, Mr. Walker. I am Detective Thompson, and this is Detective Owens," the one in front said as he was shaking my hand.

The second man, apparently Detective Owens, shook my hand but said nothing. He simply gave me a nod as he did so. Detective Thompson looked at his little pad and then spoke again.

"Sounds like you had quite the night a couple days ago. They told us about your cracked ribs," he said.

"Yeah, it was quite the night, I guess," I said.

"Is your wife feeling any better?" Thompson asked.

"No," I said. "At least, not yet."

"We're sorry to hear that," Detective Owens finally spoke up.

We were all nodding, but no one said anything for a few moments. Detective Thompson walked back to the door and was using the hand sanitizer. Detective Owens was standing by bed with his hands folded in front of his belt buckle.

"We know this is a bad time, and we have already talked extensively with a witness, but we were wondering if you could answer a few questions about what happened that night for us?" Thompson asked.

"Yes, I can answer anything you want if it help catch who did this," I said.

"That's great. Do you remember anything specific about those people who attacked you?" Thompson asked.

"There were two black men, a black woman, a black kid, and a white man. The men were all early twenties, the woman too. The kid was probably in high school," I said

"Right. Do you remember anything more specific than their race?" Thompson asked.

I sat there for a second because I didn't like the tone he used with that question. I was getting to the specifics but was opening with the generals.

"Yes, I remember more than *just their race,*" I said and my side began to hurt. "One of the black men was really strong and had big arms with tattoos on them. He is the one who hit me the most. The other black man was shorter and had on a flat brimmed hat. The woman looked kind of slutty. She had on a shirt that said "Pink" and had pretty big boobs. The white guy was skinny and looked like your typical crack head. His hair was a little longer but wasn't a full mullet yet. The kid had on a Brian Urlacher jersey but just looked like a normal kid."

Detective Thompson was taking notes in his little book, and Owens was just looking at me. He wasn't taking notes, but I could tell he was really listening.

"Did they talk to you at all?" Thompson asked and was waving his pen around while he spoke. "Did they hint as to why they did it? Was this a mutual altercation?"

"A mutual altercation?" I looked at Thompson, and he had an obvious look of curiosity on his face. I looked over at Owens, and he was staring a hole through Thompson. I looked back at Detective Thompson, and I lost it.

"Are you fucking serious? I don't know what your witness said, but this was a hate crime. My wife and I were attacked because we were white and for no other reason," I almost yelled.

"What makes you think that this was a hate crime?" Thompson asked.

"I don't know, I guess it was about the time the little one leaned down and said "Black lives matter; Bitch lives don't!" I yelled this time.

Detective Thompson stopped writing and put his pen in his pocket.

"I can see you're upset, and it will probably be better if we come back later," he said.

"Good, get the hell out of here if you're not going to do your job!" I yelled and had to double over from my side pain.

"We're sorry we caught you at a bad time, and we'll pray for you and your wife until we can speak again," Thompson said and immediately started to leave the room.

I was doubled over and had started coughing. I coughed a few more times, and tears were forming in my eyes. A nurse walked in my room and passed Detective Thompson as he left. I laid back, but Detective Owens was still by my bed. He leaned in and in a voice only I could hear he whispered, "We're going to find these guys."

That was all Owens said. He left the room and hurried to catch up to his partner. That short sentence was the first glimpse of real hope that I had all day. Before that sentence, I had received nothing but messages of faith and positivity. Detective Thompson told me that he'd pray for me. He probably wouldn't, and even if he did, is one prayer worth more than another? Does the accumulation of prayers mean more than one? People often forget that faith is not just believing; faith is an action. For three days, nothing had happened, and I was ready for some kind of action to go my way.

Chapter 12

Detective Owens

The night of June 8th

We left the hospital and headed into the parking lot. This was a smaller hospital, and there was no parking garage. Validating parking hadn't made it everywhere in Wisconsin yet. Eddie and I brought separate cars so that we could head home without going back to the station. My Dodge was parked next to his little silver Acura.

"He was a little upset," Eddie said.

I nodded, and we turned to face each other as we got to his car. There was a young couple walking towards the entrance of the hospital. The guy was about our age and had a pretty good limp. I'll never know what caused it, but the girl was helping him every step. You could tell he was embarrassed, but she wouldn't have let him take a step without her help. They made me think of the Walkers, and I had to look away.

"Wouldn't you be, too?" I asked. "His wife still hasn't woken up yet."

"I agree, but I didn't put them in that position. We're the ones trying to catch the bad guys," he said.

I nodded again. There was no reason to fight or bring anything back up. I wished it was that easy. We're the good guys, and we're after the bad guys. It was rarely that easy, and this one was blurring the lines more than most.

"What else would you have done?" He said.

I looked up, and Eddie was being sincere. He looked interested in what I thought. He was like a little brother seeking his older brother's approval. I took a deep breath and sifted through my thoughts. I could tell him that I would have sucked it up and got through interview. I could tell him that I would have understood Mr. Walker's anger. I could even tell him what I told Brian as we left. But what was the point?

"Nothing, Eddie. You handled it right. There's nothing else you could have done right now," I said. "Mr. Walker just needs some time."

Eddie couldn't help but smile and gave me a nod. He was looking for a pat on the back, and I served it up to him.

"I'll let the Captain know, and we'll see what he says," he said.

"Sounds good; G'night Eddie. I'll see you in the morning."

"Good night, Jack," Eddie said as he unlocked his Acura.

I sat in my Dodge and let Eddie leave first. I had a lot on my mind and just needed a few minutes before I headed home. I had a silver cross hanging on my rear view mirror, and I held it for a brief second before letting it swing.

I thought Brian Walker was telling the truth. I thought that the people he described were the exact people who did this to his wife and him. I had a horrible feeling that the Captain would disregard what he said for now because he came off hysterical. Upset people are always easy to push to the backburner. Once Mr. Walker calmed down, maybe enough time will have passed for us to really pursue these people. I hoped for the last part most of all. If not, I would see that justice was served, in one way or another.

Chapter 13

Detective Owens

The Morning of June 12th

I t had been four days since we met Mr. Walker. After what Eddie told him, the Captain thought it would be a good idea to give him a couple days to cool down. Imagine that: I guess I had been given the gift of prophecy but not the gift of lead detective. Throw in a weekend, and now it had been four days since we'd seen him and a week since the incident. A whole week and not one person had been arrested, and worse yet, we had no suspects.

On my own time, I went through tons of arrest reports, but Brian Walker's descriptions weren't the most specific. There were so many whitetrash, white guys in their twenties in Milwaukee that you might as well be looking for a Muslim in Yemen. Statistically, the best lead would probably come from the teenager. The problem was that he was also the least likely to have an arrest record of the group. I needed to talk to Brian more and hopefully today will be the day.

The Chief asked to see us to see him in his office at ten that morning. Of course, he told Eddie to tell me, but I was getting used to that. That Saturday, the two of them went to Joker's Bar with some other cops. I saw a picture of Eddie, Officer Coleman, Officer Bates, and the Chief on Eddie's Facebook. Officer Bates was a young African-

American woman who had been on the force for a couple years. She looked a lot like Serena Williams. She had long, curly hair that she had to wear up most of the time at work, but when she let it down, like in the picture, she was quite pretty.

The four of them had big, buzzed smiles on their faces. It was the three up and coming officers with their master, Chief Stroup. Everyone was holding a bottle of beer, and they were in front of a picture of Heath Ledger as the Joker. I didn't know if I was jealous when I saw the picture or just pissed off. It wasn't that I wanted to be in the picture with them because I probably would have declined the invitation. I'm not a sellout. I just hated the conceited nature that the picture showed. The conversations they had were probably a combination of how things used to be for the Captain and how those three officers were going to take the force to new levels if they did what the Captain told them now.

Ten o'clock rolled around, and the Captain's door opened. He stepped out, and like a sly base running coach, gave us the signal to head over. Eddie looked at me from his desk, and we gave each other the go ahead nod. Eddie puffed his chest up a little bit and did his high school strut over to the office. As I walked, I noticed two black men being interviewed at Officer Davis's desk. I paused for just a moment to look at them. One of them was very strong, but the other was tall and skinny, not short as Mr. Walker had described. They were most likely a couple of men who had been arrested last night and were getting ready to get cut loose. I shook my head and kept walking toward the Captain's office.

"Have a seat," the Captain said as we entered the room.

The first thing I saw was that damn Aaron Rodgers picture again. Just like the Facebook post, I was instantly in a worse mood seeing it. I kept my mouth shut and took my seat.

"Well, boys, you got a plan for Mr. Walker today?" He asked and raised his eyebrows as he looked back and forth between Eddie and me.

I looked over at Eddie because this was his show. I wasn't going to take any heat when I wasn't even in this puppet show. I was content with letting the puppet feel the tension for the first time since the puppet master started pulling his strings.

Eddie's face flushed a little, and then after a swallow, he began stuttering.

"We were..uh.. we were going to go see him today," he got out.

The Captain looked at him the way a teacher looks at a student who just tried hard but couldn't find the right answer. He began to nod, and I was halfway expecting him to say, "No shit, Sherlock," but he didn't make my day.

"I've been doing some thinking, and I think we need to make sure Mr. Walker remembers the right person and isn't just an upset husband," the Captain said. "Do you know what I mean?"

I honestly didn't, and so I just sat perfectly still and let Eddie nod.

"I want you to take five pictures each of people he described. We'll create a little lineup for him. So I want five white trash guys, ten black guys, five black women, and five black teenagers for him to look at," He said

"That's a good idea, Cap," Eddie chimed in.

"What if one of the real guys is in there?" I asked

"I've got that taken care of. All of the pictures will be of people who were in custody that night," he said

That wasn't a bad idea, I thought, but I just gave him an agreeing nod. Out of the corner of my eye, I noticed that Eddie had his notebook out and was taking notes. Unbelievable. He was taking ass kissing to new levels this week. I chuckled and thought that maybe he was writing a little poem for later.

> *O Captain, my Captain*
> *This storm shall pass*
> *You can stroke my ego*
> *And I'll kiss your ass*

"I want you to evaluate the way he looks at the pictures. If he immediately knows that none of them are the one, then that's good, and we'll push forward. If he looks fuzzy the whole time, then take note of that. If he picks any of them, well then, we know that we can't use that info going forward. Sound good?" he said.

"Yes sir," both of us responded.

"Good," the Chief smiled, "then get the hell out of here and get to it."

Eddie and I left the room and started putting together our file. It had taken a week, but we were finally doing something productive with this case. We were playing defense, but we were still in the game. As long as Brian Walker didn't pick someone from the file, we would switch to offense and really start looking for the people who did this.

Chapter 14

Brian

The Morning of June 12th

The rain was setting in, and it looked like it would be here all morning. I couldn't help but watch it out the window. The drops almost seemed sad as they came down. It wasn't a thunderstorm that beat the windows or a sprinkle that would not even require the windshield wipers. It wasn't the kind of rain where people talk about God crying. This wasn't a Scottish rain that came down sideways or an Arizona rain that refreshed the desert. This was a depressing Wisconsin rain. The sky was gray, and the day was calm. There was light, but the sun chose to stay away. Drop by drop, it dampened the soul. I might have been dry in Hannah's room, but the drops were soaking in just the same.

This morning was particularly hard because of what happened in the middle of the night. I woke up to nurse knocking on my door at 2:45 this morning. She tried to be polite, but her face gave her away long before the words did. Nobody knocks on your door at 2:45am unless something is wrong. She tried to cover it up with a half hearted smile, but her eyes couldn't hide the distress.

"What's wrong?" I asked before she could speak.

"Everything is ok, but we had a scare with Hannah. She's doing fine now," she said.

"What happened?" I asked.

I sat up in my bed, and for the first time didn't feel pain doing so. Tears filled my eyes, but it wasn't from pain but fear for Hannah that overcame me.

"What happened?" I asked again.

The nurse on this shift was Marge. She was a thirty-five-year-old, mother of four. We hadn't talked much in the past week besides one brief conversation about the Simpsons. She stood at the foot of my bed and took a deep breath.

"Hannah's heart briefly stopped. We were able to get the paddles and revive her very quickly. These things happen. I know it's very scary, but she is doing well now. I just felt you deserved to know. I'm sorry that it's two in the morning, but we all just felt you'd like to know that she is ok," she said professionally.

Tears were now running down my face. I used my left hand to shield my face and began sobbing. I nearly lost Hannah. As I looked up, Marge had tears in her eyes, too. The bed sheet was the nearest cloth so I used it to wipe my eyes.

"Can I see her?" I asked.

"Of course. I'll walk you over," she said

I made my way out of bed and grabbed my crutches. Over the weekend, I got out of the wheelchair. Marge and I limped down the hall to Hannah's room. The nurses looked over at us as we passed. They were all very nice, but they couldn't hide the sadness from their faces. We were like their sad movie playing out in real life, one shift at a time.

When we got to Hannah's room, I stood in the doorway. There was a nurse sitting in a chair by her. They were keeping a special eye on her after the scare. Amazingly, Hannah didn't look any different than when I saw her that evening. She was lying in bed as peacefully as ever. I walked over and grasped her hand. I watched her chest go up and down, and for the second time in minutes, I couldn't help but let the tears flow. There were two nurses in the room, but I didn't care. My wife had almost been taken from me, and I couldn't control the tears.

I sat by Hannah's bed the rest of the night. Her chest would rise and fall, the machines would beep, and nothing changed. Nurses would come and go every fifteen minutes. A few even started to ask me if I wanted to back to my room. I didn't respond to any of them. I just sat there holding her hand, and they figured out my answer.

I found myself at the window with only my thoughts. Death had been so close, and yet everything seemed the same. I had always thought of death as an event, something that comes at the end of our journey here on this earth. While watching the rain, I realized that's not the case at all. Death doesn't ride a white horse or show up with a staff. It simply comes. It doesn't wait for us to be ready or for others to say goodbye. Our schedules don't have to line up. Death is the judge, jury, and, quite literally, the executioner of our lives. Prayers don't stop it. It doesn't discriminate; it comes for the just and unjust. I just hoped this was only a scare and not a whisper that he would be coming back soon.

Chapter 15

Detective Owens

The Afternoon of June 12th

As we pulled into a parking spot at the hospital, Eddie pulled out the file we created at the station. We had enough people in custody that night that it was pretty easy to put together. The only problem was that we didn't have enough black teenagers, so we had to use two pictures of kids in juvy. Either way, it was still a good file.

"Ready?" I asked as I pulled my key out of the ignition.

Eddie had a clear look of excitement on his face. He closed the file and tucked it inside his jacket. It was raining, and he didn't want to get it wet.

"When we get in there, I'll take the lead," he said in a way that was somewhere between question and a statement.

I just nodded and pulled on my handle. The truck started to ding, and Eddie was still looking at me.

"You got it man. I'll back you up," I said and stepped out of the truck.

Eddie had put me in a position that I wasn't used to. He was the lead detective, at least on this case, but he still looked to me for assurance. I was like the former starting point guard who was supposed to help the new starting point guard on the basketball team. Just when I was about to tell him to fuck off, I ended up helping him anyways.

We stepped off the elevator and walked to Brian's room. The door was open, but when we looked, there was no one inside. A male nurse was walking by, so we he stopped him.

"Hey, is this still Brian Walker's room?" I asked.

"Yup," The man said while looking around us at the empty room.

"Do you know where he's at?" I asked.

"I'm pretty sure he's in his wife's room." He took a quick look around. "She didn't have a good night. He's been in there all day."

"Is everything ok?" Eddie asked.

"She coded last night, and we're monitoring her closely. Just keep walking down this hall, and you'll run into her room on the left," he said

"Thank you, Sir," I said and we started down the hall.

We peeked into each room as we got close. We cracked the door of the last room and saw Brian standing by the window. The door continued to open, but he never turned to face us. I let Eddie ease in front of me, and he gave a quick knock. Brian never even flinched. He just kept staring out the window. Eddie gave the typical throat clearing, "Hum, uh," and there was still no reaction. Eddie quickly looked back at me, and I returned his look with a shoulder shrug. Finally, Eddie had to speak up.

"Mr. Walker."

Brian turned his head and looked our way. He didn't look the same as he did a few days ago. As he finished facing us, I noticed how pale he now looked. He had bags under his eyes and looked tired. There was an emptiness in his eyes that I have rarely seen in my life. Everyone has a time in their life when they cry until there are no more tears left to cry. There is a short time when the sadness outlasts the tears, and I think we had walked up on Brian in that period.

Brian gestured towards the chairs in the room. There was a mini couch by the window, and he sat down on it. We sat down, and too much time passed before anyone spoke. If we were trying to avoid being awkward, that ship had sailed thirty seconds ago.

"We heard about your wife," Eddie started, "we're very sorry."

Brian just looked at his wife for a long time, then looked back to us and gave us a little nod.

"How have you been? It looks like you're moving around better," Eddie said, trying to be positive, but it only came across as ignorant because of his wife's bed being less than five feet from us.

Brian didn't respond. He just tilted his head and stared at Eddie. I didn't know if he was trying to size up Eddie's stupidity or if he, at this moment, felt bad for Eddie. All I know is that if looks could kill, we'd be a man down.

Eddie felt those eyes and sat back. He looked at me as if I had the answer. Some teachers tell you that there are no dumb questions. What a crock of shit. Asking a man how he's been when his wife nearly died last night qualifies as a stupid fucking question. Before Eddie could revert back to his high school drama days and decide to run off the stage, I stepped in.

"We are making progress, Mr. Walker," I said. "We have some pictures for you to look at if you feel up to it."

Brian moved his gaze to me and nodded. So far, he was in complete command of this room and hadn't said a word yet. I looked over at Eddie and shifted my eyes toward the file. Eddie shot up a little with an "oh yeah" movement and slid his chair over to the couch.

"We have put together a file for you to review. All of these people are potential suspects and match the description you gave us," I said as Eddie finished moving his chair.

Eddie pulled out the first group of five. It was the whitetrash lineup we created. The first man was a bulky white supremacist with "*ARYAN*" tattooed across his neck. Brian's expression never changed. He just shook his head. The next was more of the redneck, white trash variety and had a large scar continuing down from his sideburn to his jaw. It looked like he cut himself shaving with a Bowie knife. For the second time, Brian's face never changed, and he shook his head.

The third man was who I thought was going to be the closest match, and to my surprise, Brian perked up when he saw the picture. He took it from Eddie and stared at it for quite awhile. He looked up at me and back to the picture. He finally shook his head.

"I don't think this is him, but it looks a lot like him," he said and looked over at Eddie while he handed the picture back. "Like it could almost be his brother, he looks that much like him."

"But it's not him?" I asked.

"No, I don't think so," Brian said.

I was going to drop it, but Eddie had to keep poking.

"You're sure that this isn't him?" Eddie asked.

"I don't think that is the man who stabbed us, but I'd have to see him in person to be one hundred percent sure," Brian said.

"But it could be?" Eddie asked like a kid who thinks their parent is about to give in to their request.

"I guess it could be, but I'd have to see him in person," Brian said.

At that moment, I could have punched Eddie. He should have been a lawyer, not a cop. He was very good at getting people to say the thing he wanted them to say. If I knew Eddie, he'd run to the Captain and say, "He thought one of the men could have been the one, *but he'd have to see them in person to know.*" That last part would be said in a way that cast a full shadow of doubt over the whole thing. We were three pictures in, and Brian was already done. The problem was what he said, not what he meant, but it didn't matter.

We went through the rest of the file, and Brian either shook his head or said no to every picture. He took a long look at the teenagers but eventually said no to each of them. As I waited for them to finish, I looked over at Hannah. There were pictures of her and Brian sitting next to her bed. She was a very pretty lady. She looked kind, and they looked like a nice, small town couple. As I looked back to her bed, I saw her half shaven, swollen head. She was barely recognizable. She was intubated, and the machines looked like they were doing most of the work.

I looked back over to Brian. The picture of them showed a strong country man who probably was the star football player in Omro. He was probably used to stacking hay and throwing calves or whatever the hell farmers did these days. Now, he was a pale, bruised, and beaten shell of himself. The worst part was that the beating wasn't over. We had done nothing but throw invisible jabs for a week, and he was about to get a haymaker. He didn't even see it coming. Beatings don't always

59

have to be physical. The mental beating he had taken in the past twenty four hours was probably worse than the one those guys gave him a week ago. If he ever finds out that the police had "muffled" his investigation, that might be enough to push him over the edge.

When I came back to my senses, Eddie was standing up, shaking Brian's hand. Brian stayed seated.

"Thank you for your time, Mr. Walker. This was a big help," Eddie said.

I stood up and walked over to Brian. I put my hand out, and he stood up, using his crutch to push up. We were standing toe to toe. I was a little shocked at the look he had on his face.

"Something on your mind?" Brian asked looking in my eyes. "You kind of checked out there for a bit."

I had to smile on the inside a little. This guy was much sharper than I ever gave him credit for being. I wasn't sure if he would have a noticed a clown in his room earlier, but somehow he knew my thoughts had drifted for a spell.

"I just want to find the people who did this to you guys, that's all," I said.

He looked at Eddie and back to me. Our hands were still locked. The coldness was returning to his eyes even as we stood in front of each other. He just stared at me and into my eyes. I don't know if he was searching for the words to say or searching my soul. He started nodding his head, and there was nothing I could do but start to nod back. Finally he spoke.

"Alright." That was all he said as he let my hand go.

We turned and started to leave the room. I could hear Brian sit back down on the couch. Just as we were getting ready to leave his room, he spoke again.

"She didn't deserve this, you know," he said looking at Hannah.

Eddie and I stood in the doorway for a second and then left. We made our way back to the truck but those words kept playing in my head. *"She didn't deserve this."* He was right, and I didn't give a damn what others thought; I was going to try my ass off to make sure justice was served.

Chapter 16

Brian

The afternoon of June 12th

I sat on the couch looking at Hannah after the cops left. I had a lot questions and no answers. I had so many things to say to Detective Owens but couldn't find the words. He was the only one that I thought was on my side, but I couldn't say anything. A knot filled my throat, and I couldn't get the words around it.

As I looked over at Hannah, the knot wasn't budging. I noticed a picture of the two of us by her bed. It had been there for days, but this was the first time I really noticed it. I leaned back and thought of when we met. It was the first day of kindergarten, and we were a couple of scared kids who wanted their parents back. She offered me an apple at break time, and like a modern day Adam, I was hooked forever.

We grew up in the small town of Omro. It was the kind of place that some people never leave, and we ended up being those kinds of people. We knew each other and were friends through junior high, but it wasn't until high school that I started looking at Hannah with hearts in my eyes. During our junior year, Hannah went from a gangly little girl to a woman. She was like a Wisconsin Lilac. She was always there, and then one day, she bloomed; and took my breath away.

I did what every high school kid has done before: act cool and come off a fool. I remembered walking up to her by the lockers and saying the most 2000's thing to say, "Sup?" I was an idiot, and she could see right through me. She raised her eyebrows at me and laughed and mockingly returned my, "Sup?" as she pulled her last book out of her locker. I hadn't planned any further ahead, so I just stood there with a half smile that quickly turned into look of pure fear. She waited for me to say something, but I was officially frozen. Sweetly, she said, "Ok, see you tomorrow," and she walked away. When she was out of sight, I turned and fake pounded my head into a locker. I had known this girl for twelve years of my life and talked with her an unknowable number of times, but on this spring day, I couldn't even complete a sentence.

I kept trying to talk to her the rest of that week which turned into the rest of that month. My sentences became longer but had about the same substance as the first one. I would practice talking to her after school in a mirror or even while out feeding the calves. I was as cool as the other side of the pillow while I practiced. No girl would have been able to resist me. But then the end of the day would come, and I would end up like a two wheel drive pickup in the spring: stuck in the mud.

Hannah was always nice about it though. She would smile or laugh and try to seem interested for a minute before she'd leave. Unfortunately, I wasn't the only one who noticed that Hannah had changed. Other guys would talk to her and even take her on dates. These were like daggers to the heart for me. I'd see her with another guy and get the air knocked out of me. She even went to junior prom with Gary Hamilton. He was a cocky basketball player that was after

Hannah pretty hard that year. I didn't have the guts to ask her to prom, but it still hurt knowing she said yes to someone else.

My love life wasn't completely on hold at the time. I'd go on group dates with girls and was even pretty cozy with Alison Gates on prom night. My skills with the girls were improving except with the one girl I wanted, Hannah. Eventually, summer came, and I thought that I wouldn't see her for a few months. I was beside myself. What if she actually started dating Gary and I never got the chance to tell her how I really felt?

Finally, luck came my way. About a month into summer break, I was driving into town for my Dad, and who should I see but Hannah broken down on the side of the road. She had a flat tire on her blue Jeep. Like Prince Charming, I pulled over and took over changing it. I might not have been able to talk to her, but I could dang sure still change a tire. We made small talk the whole time, and to my surprise, when I finished, she gave me a big hug. Then we had a conversation that changed my life.

"I owe you big time for this," she said.

"No, no you don't owe me anything. It was my pleasure," I stumbled out.

"Well, at least let me take you to lunch for this," she said.

"No, I better get back to the farm before my Dad gets mad," I replied.

"Oh, come on, then how about dinner Friday night? You can come over; I actually cook a mean breakfast," she said smiling big now.

I laughed and blushed like a little girl but was too stupid to realize she was asking me to come hang out with her.

"No, you don't have to do that. I mean, I'd love to come over and spend the night with you but…" The words that I just said hit me and I could feel my face flush. "Not spend the night with you but spend time with you. Gosh, I'm sorry."

Hannah started laughing out loud, and if I had wings, I would have flown away. Instead, I just stood there in my typical state with her.

"Maybe we'll just start with a date before we spend the night together," she said.

"A date?" I asked.

"That's what they call it. Two people, our age, hanging out at night, right?" she said. "That is if you aren't dating Alison?"

"Yeah, I mean no, I'm not dating Alison, but yeah, that is what they call it," I said, trying to untie my words.

"Good, then do you want to go on a date with me on Friday?" She asked.

"Hell yes, I do," I blurted out, way too enthusiastically than I would have liked. I smiled and tried to cover my outburst with a new question.

"But what about Gary? Aren't you guys a thing?" I asked.

"I went to prom with him, and we've gone out a couple times, but we're not together," she said and then threw in, "yet."

"Yet?" I asked.

"Well, there is this boy that I like, but he's too scared to ask me out on a date. He comes and talks to me every day by my locker but never asks me out. I even had to ask him out to get him to come see me on a Friday night," She said, smiling, and brushed her hair out of her face. "But if he can't start talking to me, I might go ahead and call Gary."

Holy shit! The girl who I had spent countless hours thinking about and fake kissing in the mirror just told me that she liked me. She did it in kind of a mocking way, but she still said it.

"I was that obvious?" I asked.

"Oh yeah, but it was cute. That is until prom came and you didn't ask me." She rolled her eyes at me. "Then it wasn't as cute anymore. But when you kept coming around, I thought you might still have potential," she said.

I was speechless. I was smiling and slightly shaking my head. I almost didn't go into town this afternoon, and now I was going on a date with the girl of my dreams. She turned and got into her Jeep, but the door was still open.

"6:30 work for you?" She asked.

I took a couple steps and was holding her door open.

"You bet," I said.

"Perfect," she said and then came back with, "You gonna let me go now?"

"Not if I can help it," I said, and for the first time, we had a little moment. Every once in a while, life gives you little moments, and this was our first. We looked at each other, and it was the first time we did so knowing that the other felt the same.

As the memory passed, I got up and went to Hannah's bed. I picked up her hand and kissed it. There was an IV in it, but by now, it didn't faze me. I looked into her face and felt only love. We may have started out with puppy love, but now it was the kind of love that binds. "*Not if I can help it,*" I said to her and pulled my chair back up to her bed.

Chapter 17

Detective Owens

The afternoon of June 12th

"What'd you think?" I asked Eddie as we pulled out of the hospital. We were back in my truck heading toward the station.

"Man, I want to like the guy, but I don't think he really knows who did it," he said, "What do you think?"

"I don't know. I think it's worth going back again and seeing what he says a second time," I said.

"He said he thought the white guy was him. I feel bad, but he just doesn't know."

"He didn't say it was him. He said it *could* have been him," I replied.

"The guy said he thought they could have been brothers. Do you really think this guy's brother is who did this?" He went on, "He doesn't know, man."

"I know what he said, but I don't feel like that's what he meant," I said.

Eddie gave me a long look. I can usually read people fairly well, but I had no idea what was going through his head at that moment. He just stared at me with an expressionless look. If I had to guess, I'd say he was weighing out my opinion versus what the Captain would think if he said that to him. So, I went with my gut and answered the question I'm sure he was asking himself.

"What I think we should do is tell the Captain that we need one more interview to really have our answer," I said.

"You know he isn't going to like that," he said.

"I don't give a damn what he doesn't like. That's what I think we need to do." I paused, "But you're in charge, it's your call."

Eddie shook his head, rolled his eyes, and leaned back in his seat all at the same time. Eddie wanted to go back and tell the Captain what he wanted to hear so badly that it was coming out of his pores. The only thing stopping him was the fact that deep down he had to know I was right. What Brian said was most likely not what he meant. Eddie might be a self serving asshole at the moment, but he still was a young detective, and that requires a certain amount of intuition.

We pulled into the station and looked at each other. Nothing had been resolved during the trip, and this was the customary *get on the same page* time for cops. I wasn't going to speak first. Most of the time, the person who breaks first ends up losing the argument. I'll sit here all fucking day, buddy.

Finally, Eddie took a deep breath, and I could see him start to break.

"All right, I'll leave out the white man comment, but if he presses, I'm gonna tell him. You good with that?" He asked.

"I'm good with that," I responded, and we started to get out of the truck. "Hey Eddie, thanks."

We went straight to Captain Stroup's office and knocked. No one looked at us this time. I had been getting used to everyone looking at the two drama queens of the office, but they let me down this time. The office was usually pretty empty in the afternoon, and today wasn't any different.

"Come in," Captain Stroup called out.

I let Eddie go in first and followed right behind him. The Captain stood up behind his desk but didn't attempt to meet us halfway. Eddie walked over and shook his hand. I gave him a respectful nod and casually sat in one of the two chairs. Eddie took his chair next to me and the Captain sat down.

"What's the word, boys?" Captain said.

Eddie gave me a glance and then started.

"We met with Mr. Walker and showed him all of the pictures. He was pretty helpful, but not a lot came out of it." Eddie looked at me again. "Jack was thinking we should go over there one more time before we rule his opinion out or not."

The Captain looked over at me. His look couldn't hide the new, annoyed state we had just placed him in.

"What makes you say that?" he asked.

"Mr. Walker went through the pictures and pretty much knew every one of them immediately wasn't them. I just figured to be safe, we should do it one more time," I said.

"What do you mean by "pretty much"?" Captain asked.

"I just meant that he didn't immediately know them all but that most of them he did, so he *pretty much* knew them all," I said.

"What do you mean, he didn't immediately know them all?" The Captain sat up in his chair. "Did you try and coach him, or did he not know?" Captain said.

"I didn't try and coach him at all. Eddie asked the questions, and he did not try to coach him either. We just showed him the pictures, and he said what he thought. I just think one more time would put the department in a better position at the end of the day."

The Captain sat back in his chair and was soaking up what I just said. He was looking at me for a few seconds, nodding his head. He looked down at a piece of paper on his desk and then back up at us. The way he was nodding made me think that we might walk out of here on a high note. Then, one statement changed everything.

Eddie spoke up, and my chest tightened.

"There was one thing, Captain. Mr. Walker thought that one of the white guys could have been him. Now I agree with Jack, but he did say that. Specifically, he said that it looked so much like him that they could be brothers, but he needed to see him person to know."

The Captain looked at Eddie and then over at me, and his head was starting to turn red.

"You didn't think that was pertinent information?" he rhetorically asked in my direction. "You gotta be fucking kidding me."

"You weren't there Captain..." I started.

"Did he say it or not?" The Captain interrupted.

I just sat there and stared at him. We were ten seconds from walking out of there, and Eddie completely screwed the pooch.

"He did say it, Captain," Eddie chimed in.

"You're really starting to slip, Owens. This whole case has been like a one fuck up after another for you," The Captain said.

"Cut the shit, Captain." I couldn't take it anymore. "I was sitting there, not you. I know what I heard and more importantly what I saw. This guy could identify who did this, and we owe him one more shot."

"Watch your fucking mouth, Owens. Don't you ever speak to me like I'm some common cop. I'm your fucking Captain, and don't you forget it."

"I'm not the one forgetting things around here. Or as you might say *muffling* things. All I'm trying to do is find who did this. Maybe if all three of us were on board with that, we'd get somewhere."

"You shut the fuck up and get out of my office. Don't you ever insinuate that shit."

"I'm not insinuating anything. I don't want anything to do with you or your little puppet." I gave a thumb gesture toward Eddie.

The Captain slammed his fist down on the desk. His Aaron Rodgers picture fell over. There is no doubt that everyone heard it outside. But at that point, I didn't care. I was standing up for what was right, and I wasn't backing off now.

"I'll tell you what. You're suspended. I'm going to give you a week off to think about your position here. This way, I don't fire your ass right now," Captain said, more calmly than I was expecting. "Now like I said, get the fuck out of my office."

If you've ever been benched and thought the coach was wrong for doing it, then you have a glimpse of what I was going through. The difference was that I was being benched for an ass kisser and I didn't do anything wrong to begin with. I stood up and purposefully gave the

71

Captain a "fuck you" stare and then turned and walked out. I didn't even make an attempt to look at Eddie. I did make sure to slam the door behind me to emphasize the "fuck you" I was trying to send.

When I left his office, I was greeted by every set of eyes in the station. I didn't try to return their gaze. They were going think what they wanted and by the time I got back, everyone will have their minds made up about the situation. Unfortunately for me, all the info would be from those two, so I was sure they would think I was in the wrong. I walked to my desk and started to gather my things. There was a paper on my desk with Ms. Martinez's number on it. It was a small step, but I grabbed it anyway. This week wasn't going to be wasted.

Chapter 18

Brian

The Morning of June 13th

It had been about thirty hours since I'd slept. I was not tired though. At least not in the way that I was used to being tired. I doubted I could go to sleep even if I tried. I felt like I was hungover but worse. My body had started to ache in my core but only when I moved. If I sat still, I didn't really feel anything. Sometimes, my hands felt like they were shaking, but when I stopped and look at them, they weren't. My body felt like a house full of lights, and they were taking turns flickering.

My eyes were the worst. They were heavy, but the pain came from behind my eyeball. I thought, cried, and thought some more. I had done this for so long that I didn't want to think anymore. Hannah used to get mad at me for leaving my contacts in for too long. If she woke up, she'd be pissed at me. I was at the point where I didn't know if they were in or not. I didn't remember taking them out, but there was a blur forming around the outside of everything I saw. I would go check in the mirror but that would require me walking to the bathroom, and I didn't want to do that. One: I didn't want to move. And Two: I didn't want to look at myself right now.

I hated to admit it, but in a morbid way, this almost felt good. For a week, I had to watch Hannah be in a terrible state while I got better. At least now, I got to feel something besides guilt. I knew that there was nothing that I could have done differently, but that didn't matter. I was like the soldier who didn't get shot. Why me and not them? Was God looking out for me, or did He just forget about Hannah?

I had started to convince myself that there was no God. I wasn't sure if I believed it yet, but the seed was growing. If one of us had to be on the verge of dying, it should be me. Fate is knowing that the main character dies and then wrapping it in bullshit. As fate would have it, someone placed a Bible on the corner of the couch. Fate and irony must be kissing cousins.

I pushed the Bible and heard it thud as it hit the floor. Just as I expected, nothing happened. I laid my head back and closed my eyes. I took my thumb and started pushing on my ribs. As the pain shot up my body, I dug harder. I pushed hard enough that my cheek twitched, and I started to double over. I began coughing and opened my eyes. Tears had come back but weren't falling yet. I squeezed my fist together and dug my nails into my palm. I used my thumb to push harder. When I opened my hand, I hand four fingernail lines in my palm but no blood.

"I'm sorry, Hannah," I said to her, "I'm sorry. This shouldn't have happened. I should be there not you."

I sucked my bottom lip in between my teeth and started to bite down. Tears welled in my eyes, and I bit harder. I closed my eyes and drove down harder until I could feel my two front teeth sink into blood. I had bit off a small piece from the inside of my bottom lip. I leaned over and spit it on the Bible. Blood was coming out of my mouth now, and I spit it behind the couch.

The Marines say that pain is weakness leaving the body. My slogan would be pain is better than guilt. At least right now it was. I looked over at Hannah, and it was like she was looking at me. She hadn't moved, and her eyes were closed, but I could feel her looking at me. Blood was trickling down my chin, and for the first time, I felt something different: shame.

"I know, Babe. I'm sorry," I said out loud to her again.

I stood up and walked into the bathroom. I stood in front of the mirror and watched the blood fall into the sink. I grabbed a rag and dampened it. When I placed it on my inner lip, I instantly knew that was a bad idea. I threw the rag down and grabbed a plastic cup. I proceeded to take sips, swish it around, and spit it out. The blood thinned as I repeated this over and over again. When it stopped bleeding, I looked in the mirror. I had a week old beard and was dirty. My face was less swollen, but I still looked beat up. I grabbed both sides of the sink and looked closely at my eyes. *"I should be laying there,"* I said to myself out loud.

When I walked back into her room, I walked over and held Hannah's hand. She never moved, but I knew she saw me. I don't know how, but I could feel her eyes.

"I'm sorry, Babe. I'll try to control my fits," I said and smiled because she used to tell me to "control my fits" all the time.

"I'll try to do better for you."

I leaned down and kissed her hand. I would have given the world just to feel her squeeze it back.

"I know I need to, Babe. I'll lie down on your couch, but I'm not leaving. I'll just be right there," I said.

I walked over to the couch and laid down. Hannah never said a word, but she didn't have to. We had been together long enough that I knew what she'd say. I could even hear the way that she'd say it. She'd want me to get some sleep, so I closed my eyes. I'd be damned if I was going back to my room, though. I was not going to leave my Hannah.

Chapter 19

Detective Owens

The Afternoon of June 13th

Day one of my suspension had not been very successful. I stopped by the liquor store last night and picked up a bottle of Jack Daniels. It's amazing how much a man can drink when you know there's nothing to wake up for in the morning. Once I woke up, I felt the after effects, but I guess if you're gonna dance, you have to the pay the band.

My apartment was filthy. I hadn't been in it much in the last week, but holy shit. I needed a maid. Dishes were stacked up, clothes were everywhere, and there was a pizza box on my coffee table. My apartment consisted of two bedrooms, a living room, a kitchen, and a small bathroom. Everything was dirty except for my spare bedroom. Since my ex-girlfriend moved out six months ago, I had only been in there about three times. This is where I'd set up my work station.

I took out Ms. Martinez's number and thumb tacked it into the white wall. It wasn't much, but it a was start. Every investigation has to start somewhere. One pebble can start the ripple. I stepped back and looked at my lone piece of paper. This was a pretty big puzzle, and all I had was a single phone number. I went to the kitchen because I didn't even have a chair in that room. I brought back one of my two kitchen chairs and a piece of paper.

I needed to make a to-do list for this case. First, I needed to contact Ms. Martinez and have a real interview. The last one that she sat through was more of an interrogation and didn't lead to any new leads. Maybe if I was alone, she would be willing to talk to me again. Second, I needed to get my hands on Big Jimmy's surveillance tapes to see if I could get a plate number off the white car. Third, I needed to go see Mr. Walker and get any details that might have been overlooked. I felt a weird connection to this guy, and I thought that he felt the same. Mr. Walker might just think that Eddie was a piece of shit and I was the better alternative, but at this point, I would take it.

The hardest part about this will be trying to gather information without any other cops finding out. They couldn't know what I was doing, or I would be Grade A fucked. Luckily, the Captain was so pissed that I walked out with my badge and gun. People are always a little more willing to talk when you flash the badge. I would give Ms. Martinez a chance to get home from work. I didn't know if she had a job, but it would probably be polite to assume that she did. I thumb tacked my freshly written piece of a paper next to the other and left the chair in the vacant room.

I walked back into the living room and turned on the television. I hadn't watched it since the Captain's interview on The O'Reilly Factor, so it was still on Fox News. I was getting ready to flip it to Sportscenter when I saw the headline flash across the bottom of the screen. *Six dead in Cleveland riot.* It went to commercial, but I decided to wait. After watching reasons to buy gold and to buy the latest political thriller, the news came back on.

Last night, a cop killed an eighteen year old black kid, and now Cleveland was in full on riot mode. An official report of what happened had not been released, but a six second video shot with a camera phone showed the cop shooting the young man. I leaned back on my couch and shook my head. Same shit, different chapter. Once the video surfaced, the town erupted like a volcano. Cop cars were on fire, shops looted, and it basically looked like a scene from an apocalypse movie.

The worst part was that one of the shops was owned by a small family, and they fought back as the looters tried to force their way in. They shot two of them while they were in the store, and the others set the store on fire. The family consisted of a husband, his wife, and their nineteen year old son. All three of them were trapped and burned inside the store. The news believed that the two they shot were dead before the fire, but they have yet to be pulled from the remains. One other police man was shot on the same street about an hour after the shop incident.

This was becoming unbelievable. The country was wobbling, and everyone was waiting for it to fall. Half the country wanted it to fall, and the other half was trying hold it up. The problem was that each thought they were the one holding it up. I couldn't help but shake my head on the couch. Then the pictures of all the people involved in the shop incident came up, and at this point, nothing would surprise me.

There were two obvious gangbangers, the ones shot while they were looting who were both black. There pictures were former mug shots. Then there was a family picture of the store owners, taken in front of their shop. The husband was a heavier, clean cut, black man; his wife was a short, blonde haired, white woman; and their son was a combination of the two except he wore glasses. This was your average, everyday American family who had been attacked because their small shop had been in the wrong place.

The next topic on Fox News made me sick and say, "Fuck you" out loud to my television. It was going to be about whether all of these people would still be alive if we had stricter gun laws. I shut my television off and pondered how we had become so stupid to really believe some of this shit. The Walkers were in the hospital, and no guns were involved. Guns don't just fire themselves. I have five guns in my house, and I have yet to kill anyone. If I wanted someone dead, it starts with a thought. The thought becomes action, and that action can end with a gun shooting someone. Taking away the guns is the last step in the process. If they want to change the way things are, then change the way people think. The way my thoughts were going lately, I probably needed to follow my own advice.

Chapter 20

Brian

The evening of June 13th

I woke up to a loud noise and four nurses rushing into Hannah's room. The last nurse wheeled a cart in and went to the side of Hannah's bed. For a second, I was confused. I couldn't understand what the rush was about, and then I heard it. Hannah had flat lined, and there was a constant beep. One of the nurses came up to me.

"Mr. Walker, we need to get you out of here," she said

She reached for my arm to help me up, but I snatched it away. I was sitting upright now. I leaned back toward the corner of the couch like a little kid.

"I'm not leaving," I scolded. "Help Hannah."

The nurse looked helplessly at the doctor who was now in the room. The doctor looked at me and said, "Keep him over there."

This wasn't Dr. Shapour. I had met this doctor once this week though. She was one of the few female doctors I had seen at the hospital and was very direct the one time we met.

The nurse grabbed my arm and sat on the couch beside me. She may have been trying to appear consoling, but she was there to leash me to the couch. I didn't care because my eyes were now fixed on Hannah.

This was a real life version of Grey's Anatomy. I heard the doctor say "Clear," and everyone took a step back except the one with the paddles. I could see Hannah's body jolt, but nothing happened afterward. She commanded them to "turn it up a notch" and yet again let out a "Clear," and there was another jolt. This time, I looked at the nurse who was assigned to me, and she tried to ease my mind.

"They're doing everything they can, Mr. Walker. It'll be ok," she said, but I could see a shade of doubt.

I looked back to the bed and the doctor was hurling another command. "Once more," she said and followed it with another "Clear." For a third time, Hannah's body jolted up and came back down. For a moment, no one in the room moved. The nurse squeezed my arm. We all wanted that machine to start beeping.

"Come on, Babe," I whispered.

I don't know if she heard me, but at the exact instance, the machine started beeping again. I could feel the collective sigh that followed. Everyone was holding their breath, and Hannah had given it back. I looked over at the nurse sitting next to me, and with tears in her eyes, she smiled. She started to pat my arm where she had been holding it. There were no words to say at this moment, and that pat was sufficient.

The lady doctor walked over to the couch, and I could see her name badge. Her name was Dr. Jenkins. She smiled and took an exaggerated deep breath.

"That was a close one, but we're not going to let her sneak away like that." She said.

"Thank you, Doc. I was sleeping on the couch and didn't know anything was happening until everyone rushed in," I said.

"That's ok. That's what we're here for." She took a long look at me. "Maybe you should go get some rest in your own room for a bit. I can have a nurse give you updates if you'd like."

I nodded. Even if I didn't like it, she was right.

"Andrea, will you walk him back to his room?" She asked the nurse who was next to me.

"Yes," she answered. "Are you ready Mr. Walker?"

I nodded again and stood up. As we started to leave, I paused next to the foot of Hannah's bed. She didn't look any different than she did that morning, and yet she had almost died minutes ago. I started to feel a knot swell in my throat. I came into her room thinking I was going to protect her. A lot of good that did. If Hannah's going to make it, it's going to be because of her sheer will to live at this point. *Keep fighting, babe. Please keep fighting.*

Chapter 21

Detective Owens

The night of June 13th

Once I finished my George Foreman Grill hamburger, it was time to call Ms. Martinez. I went into my spare bedroom and sat down at the lone chair. I thought I might have gas from the burger, but butterflies were starting to flutter in my stomach. Teenage boys will get ready for battle when they call their little crush. They'll psych themselves up and hope that they sound as cool on the phone as they do in the mirror just moments before. I wasn't to this level, but I did practice saying "Hello" before I actually dialed and had to say "Hello" for real. As I pushed send, I let out an exhale. It's go time.

The phone rang and rang and rang, and I'll be a son of bitch if it didn't go to voicemail. I hung up because I wasn't prepared for that. Damn it. I didn't even think about her not answering, but there was no way I could leave a message. I might as well leave a perfect evidence trail right up to my door if I do that. I leaned my head to the left and popped my neck. I started to look at my paper on the wall. I probably should call her one more time in an hour or so and hope she picked up. Just as I was about to stand up, my phone started to ring. There was no name, just a number with a Milwaukee area code. I looked back up to the wall and it was Ms. Martinez's number. I cleared my throat.

"Hello" I answered.

"Did you call me?" a female voice responded.

"Yes, this is Detective Owens. Please don't hang up. I have just a couple of questions for you."

There was a pause. She must have deciding if she wanted to talk or give me the double screw you by hanging up.

"Ms. Martinez, are you there?" I asked breaking the silence.

"Ya, I'm here. What do you want?"

"I just have a few follow up questions from our interview the other day."

"Sorry Officer, I don't think I remember what happened anymore," she said before my questions started.

"If I showed you a picture, would you be able to identify someone from that night?"

Immediately she said, "No."

"Had you ever seen any of them in the neighborhood before that night?

"No."

"Would you be able to look at just one picture if I brought it by?"

"No."

"Ma'am, those people are still in the hospital, would you at least try?" I asked, hoping to get some kind of empathy from her.

"I'll tell you what, how about you have Officer Thompson look at them because I don't remember shit. In fact, give him a message for me." Her voice was starting to rise. "You can write this down if you'd like. Tell him to go FUCK himself."

And just like that, the phone was dead. I said her name, but there was no one on the other end. I pushed redial, but it went straight to voicemail this time. The bridge was officially burned. We had hurt her pride, and there was no way she was going to help us now. I leaned forward and crossed her name off my short list.

Truthfully, I don't blame her. It made my job harder, but I still don't blame her. Nothing made me angrier than being treated like a second rate citizen or a dumbass. We had accomplished both in one sitting with her.

In the morning, I would head over to Big Jimmy's and see if I could get my hands on their surveillance tapes. I know the odds were they were in the Captain's office, but they might have made a copy. I could at least hope right now. Until then, I was going to head back into the living room and talk philosophy with my good friend, Jack Daniels. My glass was currently half empty, and his bottle was half full. When your world is going to hell, no one has an ear like Gentleman Jack.

Chapter 22

Brian

The morning of June 14th

My eyes opened, and Hannah was in front of me. She had on a beautiful white dress, and her haired was curled. It wasn't a fancy white prom dress but something a girl might wear in the late spring or early summer. She was smiling and waving at me to come with her. As we walked, I looked around and recognized that we were on our ranch in Omro.

The grass was always so green in the summer, and this was the greenest I'd ever seen. It came up to my shins and was lush. The surrounding trees looked vibrant and full. I felt like I was in a picture of Eden. There are perfect Wisconsin summer days on occasion, and this must have been one of them. There weren't any cows in sight. I did see a deer at the edge of the tree line, and it casually walked away as we approached.

My mind was somewhere between phases. I knew that this wasn't real, but it felt like the wind that touched my skin was more than a thought. It may have been a memory, but that didn't feel right, either. It was the kind of dream that you don't want to wake from. Hannah was still in front of me but repeatedly turned back to me and smiled.

"Wait for me, Babe," I said out loud, but she couldn't hear. Then it hit me. There was no sound. All of this beauty, but I couldn't hear anything.

"Babe," I called out louder, but there was still no sound. Hannah just smiled at me. Her mouth began to move, but her voice was lost. She tilted her head at me, the way she always did, and smiled. I reached for her hand, and she shook her head.

I looked back toward the forest and saw the flowers blooming. Giant sunflowers, Hannah's favorites, were scattered around the field. There was a sea of purple, pink, red, and yellow around us now. They were all flowers that I had gotten for Hannah at some point. Roses bloomed at our feet that had I had never seen on the ranch before.

When I raised my gaze toward Hannah again, she was holding a daisy. She kissed it and let the wind take it away. Then we just looked at each other. Both of us had tears in our eyes, not out of sadness but because this may have been the happiest time of my life. This was no memory. She began to speak again, but there still no sound. I could start to make out what she was saying though. I wasn't reading her lips or hearing her words. I could feel them in my heart as if she was penning them there.

She said that she loved me. At that moment, I knew more than ever that she did. She said she wished that we had more time. In the instance of a blink, I was able to see most of our entire lives together. The little hugs and touching moments filled up the most time. She said that she had to go.

I began to plead with Hannah not to go. She just shook her head. She turned and started to walk away.

"Please," I begged her.

She turned again and pointed to her necklace. She told me that she'd always be with me. I had given her that necklace years ago, and Hannah wore it every day. I hadn't even noticed that she had it on. It wasn't fancy; it was just a sterling silver pendant of a heart. She loved it though, and even now, in the midst of all this beauty, she still had it on.

She glanced toward the distance and looked back toward me. She said it was time for her to go now. She pointed to her heart and said she was going to be ok. As the words wrapped themselves around my heart, I knew she would be. She smiled and started to walk toward the distance. I let her go, and when I did so, my hearing came back.

"Mr. Walker," my nurse Kelly said as I awoke. She had tears running down her face. She leaned over and dabbed her eyes with the sleeve of her scrub. I watched as she composed herself and tried to speak again.

"Mr. Walker, I am so sorry to have to tell you this but…" The tears came again.

I touched Kelly's hand. She looked up at me and was doing everything she could not to cry.

"I know," I said. That was all I needed to say. I was not crying or emotional. To tell you the truth, the peace from my dream or whatever that had been was still in my heart.

"Can I see her?" I asked.

Kelly couldn't control herself anymore and began to sob.

"I'm sorry, Mr. Walker, I 'm so sorry."

I moved my calming hand to her shoulder. I started to pat her shoulder in a consoling matter. In the moment that should have shattered me, I was looking out for someone else. Hannah had rubbed off on me more than I thought.

Kelly finally gained control of herself and after a tissue said, "Yes, sir. You may see her if you'd like."

I nodded and got out of bed. I walked down the hallway, and every nurse in the hospital looked at me while I walked. I don't think they meant to, but their sad movie had just ended, and there wasn't a surprise happy ending after all.

As I entered into her room, two nurses gave me their sympathies and left. Hannah looked peaceful. She was not the beauty that I had seen just minutes ago, but I believe that wherever she was, she was that beautiful now. This was Hannah's body, but I believed I saw her soul. I went over and held her hand.

"Thank you for saying goodbye. I don't know how I'm going to keep going, but thank you for stopping in. I'll never forget that. You are the love of my life," I said and felt love, not pain. The pain would come but not right now. "I love you, Hannah."

I leaned forward and kissed her lips and then her forehead. There was one thing I needed before I left. There was a bag of Hannah's personal items under the dresser. I went through it until I found a little heart necklace. I kissed it and slid it over my head. She would always be with me.

Chapter 23

Detective Owens

The morning of June 14th

Big Jimmy's was just like every other local garage that I've been to in my life. As I walked up, I accessed the scene. There were three guys standing around an old 1980's soda machine talking while another one was under a lifted car. They were all white, but their ages ranged quite a bit. The oldest had to be in his mid-sixties and wore a shitty little rat tail that some would call a pony under his sweat stained baseball cap. Then there was a fat man with a greasy beard who was probably in his early fifties. His clothes were unusually dirty for it being so early. My guess was that they never get cleaned, and the large body underneath them wasn't too far behind. The third man standing with them was in his early twenties. Most likely, he was the kid who killed it in shop class but forgot that there was more to life than cars. I could see that his entire left arm was a sleeve of skull tattoos and car logos.

"How's it going today?" I asked as I strolled up. They all looked at me like I had just interrupted their break time.

"It's going," the fat man spoke up.

There is nothing worse than feeling like the new kid in school and nobody wants to talk to you. I almost just started asking my questions, but I needed them to cooperate. I had to find some common ground, and the poster on the wall gave me that. Nothing brings men together more than a naked lady on the wall.

"Damn, she'll get you up for work in the morning," I said laughing.

All three men started laughing and nodding their heads. The fat man gestured at the old man.

"For Bill, it's more of a hold up than a stick up." He could barely get it out through his laughing.

"Fuck you, Jerry," The old man came back with a smile. "At least I've seen mine this year."

"I don't have to see it. That's Kyle's mom's job!" Jerry came back and slapped the kid on the back.

All of a sudden, a voice came from under the lifted car.

"Get off Kyle's mom, Jerry, and I'll get off yours."

Every one was cracking up in the garage. It's funny how no matter how old men get, the high school humor never gets old. Once the laugh was over, the fat man spoke up again, but this time with an entirely different tone.

"I'm Jerry. What can we do for you?"

"I'm Detective Owens, and I was wondering if I could take a look at your surveillance tapes."

"Damn, you boys sure do like to take a look at our tapes. What happened this time?" The old man, Bill, said.

"Nothing new. I just need to see the tape from June fifth."

Jerry wiped his hands on a filthy rag and threw it down on some tools. I took a better look at his dirty overalls and was actually impressed. As he turned to throw the rag, I noticed that his back was just as dirty as his front. There was barely a square on his overalls that didn't have a grease stain on it.

"Well buddy, I don't think we can help you there. One of your comrades came by and picked that tape up already," Jerry said.

"He never brought it back?" I asked.

"Nope, ain't seen him since," Jerry replied.

"You wouldn't happen to have a copy would you?" I asked, even though I knew the answer.

Jerry looked at me like I was crazy.

"No, we're not the Pentagon around here. Truthfully, you're lucky we had one copy, let alone two."

"Just figured I'd ask." I took a breath and looked around. Big Jimmy's was surprising a clean shop. Every tool had its place, and the floor was even swept. The dirtiest part of the shop was the employees.

"Why don't you ask the guy who came in here?" Jerry asked.

"I'll have to." I could see that Jerry was wondering why I hadn't already. "It's just that I won't see him for a few days: department bullshit."

They all nodded like they knew what I was talking about. They didn't, but everyone can relate to bullshit. That is the working man's bond. When you're not at the top, which few of us are, then we all have to put up with bullshit. Tapping into that relationship never hurts your case. I was just getting ready to leave when the old man, Bill, spoke up.

"You catch them niggers who beat them white folks up yet?"

Even in a blue collar garage, that word had sting to it. I'm pretty neutral on race, but I hate that word. I think that whether you're white or black, the people who use it in a demeaning way are ignorant.

"Still looking," I responded coldly. "Well, thanks guys. I appreciate your time. Don't go blind looking at that poster."

Everyone started laughing, and I left through the big open door. Another lead that shriveled up before it went anywhere. That means I'm 0 for 2 and only have one chance left. I got into my truck and looked at my phone. If I headed over to the hospital, I would be able to get there before lunch. Hopefully, Mr. Walker was having a good day, and I would be able make some progress.

Chapter 24

Brian

The late morning of June 14th

"Are you sure you won't stay?" Dr. Shapour asked.

"Yes, I'll be leaving as soon as I'm packed," I said and stuck out my hand, "Thank you for everything you did while we were here."

Dr. Shapour had tried for ten minutes but could tell that I was going to leave and finally submitted by shaking my hand. He didn't speak the best English, but he was a very good doctor, and I could tell that he cared about Hannah and me.

"If you have any questions, please don't hesitate to call me," he said and left the room.

Once he left the room, I started to get dressed in my normal clothes. As I put my pants on, I realized I needed a belt. I had been in the hospital for nine days, and my clothes were significantly looser. Living on hospital Jell-o and fear was an easy way to lose a lot of weight. I looked through the bag that Hannah's mom brought several days ago, but there was no belt. I guess it didn't really matter anyways.

My room was empty besides me and my television. This was a rarity during my stay, but after my talk with Doctor Shapour, I doubted anyone would bother me. When a person's mind is truly made up, it's best to just get out of the way. My recovery meant nothing to me anymore. I wasn't going to die, and if I did, I wouldn't complain. Now that Hannah was gone, all I wanted was to get home as fast as I could.

My things were just about packed when CNN flashed *Breaking News* across the screen. I paused to see what other horrible thing happened in the world today. In my time here, I had learned how truly horrible life was for most people. I used to not watch the news, but I had found that it's a better soap opera than any day time drama could hope to be. Now that my life had lost its purpose, I found the news much more interesting.

Cleveland Cops Refuse to Act was the headline. I turned up the volume to listen. During the course of the most recent Black Lives Matter riot, many police officers refused to pursue black criminals. Victims were in an outrage. An anonymous tip to the media, believed to be within their own police department, led to this discovery. The Cleveland police department had refused to comment at this moment.

Holy shit. I was in shock looking at the screen. I just stood by my bed as commercials flashed in front of me. This couldn't be right, could it? A reporter came back on and began speaking.

"The story is that a few cops refused to arrest some criminals because of their race. More importantly, they didn't want to "ruffle any feathers right now," the reporter air quoted with her hands. "Several purse snatchings have occurred in the last twenty four hours, and the cops have made no effort to apprehend the suspects. Finally, a member of the police department called up the local media and gave the real reason why nothing has happened with these crimes. He went on to say, 'When they quit rioting, then we'll find these guys'."

Nine days and nothing had been done about Hannah's killer. This couldn't be happening here, could it? I shook my head. There is no way; cops don't work like that. Then again, it made sense. I had met with the cops twice and both meetings had an odd feeling. The younger looking cop seemed to be looking for a way out every time we met. Son of a bitch.

I needed to talk to Detective Owens before I left. He was the only one that I semi-trusted right now. I looked by my table, but there was no card. I couldn't remember if he'd left one or not. I walked to the other side of the bed and looked, but there was still nothing. I wouldn't have left it in the bathroom, but I guessed it was worth a look. As I walked, I couldn't stop wondering if this was what happened to Hannah and me. Were we the victims in Milwaukee? As I stepped into the bathroom, I heard a knock at the door.

Chapter 25

Detective Owens

The late morning of June 14th

I knocked on Brian Walker's door but didn't see anyone inside. A nurse stopped me as I was approaching his door, and she informed me about his wife's passing. I felt horrible and almost left to give him some time by himself. But then she told me that he was planning on leaving this afternoon. She informed me on all the nurses' thoughts, and I thanked her. Gossip spreads like wildfire, and in a contained space, like a hospital, it spreads even faster.

Brian walked out of the bathroom and looked stunned to see me. I didn't blame him after everything he had gone through. His room was empty except a bag on his bed. As he walked toward me, he began to speak.

"Come in."

I walked in and swung the door shut behind me. Now that we were closer, I could see how strung out Brian looked. His clothes hung off his body, and he looked feeble. His blue jeans didn't fit anymore, and his white t-shirt made him look like someone's younger brother. This was a strong country man when he came in but now the phrase "rode hard and put up wet" came to mind. I couldn't even begin to image what he was going through. I'd never been married and at this pace probably never would be. I was sympathetic to his loss, but without any real experience, it was hard to be truly empathetic.

"I'm sorry for your loss," I started and immediately wished it would have come out better.

He nodded at me but did not answer. I was sure he had heard that so many times in the last few hours that there was no need to reply anymore. It was still one of those things a person has to say. You're either a dipshit for saying it or you can be a dick for not. I'd rather not be a dick.

"Brian, I know there couldn't be a worse time, and if you don't want to talk right now, I completely understand. I can leave my card for later if you need me to. But the nurses said you were leaving and there are a couple things I'd like to ask before you leave."

"That's no problem," Brian said easily, "There's actually a couple things I'd like to ask you, too."

"No problem. What's on your mind?" I replied.

"You watch the news?" he asked.

"Sometimes but not all the time," I answered.

"You see it today?"

"No," I said and began to feel a little uncomfortable.

He pointed up toward his television on the wall. There had been enough coverage on Cleveland lately that I knew that was the background. Then he turned it up so that the volume was at its max. A woman was being interviewed and appeared upset. She looked like your classic sit on the porch and drink tea all day citizen. The shirt she had on matched many shower curtains that I've seen in my life.

"I don't understand why they won't arrest them just because they're black. That's the most racist thing I've ever heard," she proclaimed during her two minutes of fame.

The television got muted, and I looked back toward Brian. He was staring at me with the remote in his hand. He didn't say anything. I felt like a high school kid whose parents just found his porn stash and now they're waiting for you to explain yourself. Words don't mean much at this point. An awkwardly long time passed before Brian broke the silence.

"I don't have a lot to say, Detective Owens. But was there anything like this going on here? Is this why no one has been arrested yet?" He asked.

I thought long and hard about my answer. Part of me wanted to throw Eddie and the Captain under the bus. They were behind this, not me. I had done nothing wrong. I also knew that it would cost me my career if I did so.

"Brian, I can promise you that I did everything in my power to try and catch these people. And I promise you that I will continue to do so until justice is served," I said.

"I believe you. I want to believe you. But what about everyone else?" he asked.

My collar got tight. How could I stand here and lie to this man who has lost everything? I looked down at the remote he was holding. If he squeezed it any harder, the thing would explode.

"I can't speak for everyone. I can only tell you that I have tried and will never stop trying to bring these people in."

Brian took a deep breath and closed his eyes. He knew what I meant, and the words were sinking in. He dropped the remote on the bed and picked up his bag. He slung it over his shoulder, and we stood there looking at each other.

"Do you believe in the Bible?" He asked.

"Yes." I said.

"I don't." He shook his head. "At least not anymore, but I do believe they got it right in the beginning. Before the love your neighbor bullshit, it was an eye for an eye. So if you do find them, don't bring them in. Kill 'em."

He started walking toward me and even stuck out his hand. Out of instinct, I shook it. He stopped, and we were a foot away from each other.

"And if you can't do it, send them to me." Brian said.

He left the room and I took a deep breath. I could still feel the hatred in his handshake. Truthfully, I didn't blame him. I felt more alive in that handshake than I'd felt for a long time. I told myself, "I'm going to try my best to find these people, not for his sake, but for theirs." God only knows what he'd do if he got a hold of them.

Part 2

Chapter 1

2015

Brian

The Night of June 4th

I became a big fan of Voodoo. Not the bullshit from New Orleans that involved dolls and swamps. I'm talking about the glorious combination of Vodka and Mountain Dew. This had become my new best friend. I'd split my glass 60/40 and let it take care of the rest. I used to drink Coors Light, but about six months ago, my drinking was placed into quite the predicament. I was starting to get full before I'd get drunk. This forced me to find a harder liquor, and I didn't look back.

Tomorrow was the anniversary of Hannah's attack. I was going to visit her grave, and to prepare myself, I decided to drink all day. Some might call it liquid courage, but that wasn't why I did it. I drank for the numbing effect. When I visited her grave without it, I would always lose control. The tears would flow down my face until my cheeks quivered. The hole in my heart got wider, and it would physically hurt. When I visited her grave after drinking, the hole widened, but the tears didn't flow.

By four o'clock, my vision was blurred. I was still able to feed the horses and count the chickens. Hannah loved her chickens, and I'd kept them going for the past year. She had twenty egg laying hens, and all but one of them had made it. Last winter, one of the hens got out and froze to death. I hated those chickens when Hannah was alive, but I buried that hen in the middle of January. I had to use the backhoe bucket because of the frozen ground, but she got buried nonetheless.

By seven o'clock, my balance was wobbling. Most of the night was spent looking at a few old pictures on my couch, so it didn't matter. The end table was now home to every photo album that we had. It was mostly wedding pictures, but there were a few taken after that as well. My favorite picture was the one of the two of us on our old red tractor. My grandpa bought it forty five years ago, and it still ran. We had a newer tractor, but we kept the old one because Hannah loved it. It was a sunny, spring day and we were cleaning the barn. It shouldn't have been a good time to take a picture, but she looked so happy. She had a huge smile, and her arms were wrapped around me. That picture captured our everyday life together perfectly. I'd bought one picture frame in my whole life, and it was for that picture. I was afraid that I'd ruin it from holding it every night.

My watch said it was nine o'clock now, and I needed a shower. I had three days of Voodoo coming out of my pores. I smelled like a homeless man who happened to camp at a farm for a few days. As I stood up to go to the shower, the floor moved. I stumbled into the nearby chair, and the floor moved back the other way. I felt like I was on a ship, and the waves were getting bigger. The floor kept swaying and as I centered myself I thought I might puke. This was not normal, and I knew that I drank too much.

Once I got to the bathroom, I started to fill the tub. Bathing while intoxicated can be a little tricky. You can either shower and risk falling down through the curtain, or you can take a bath and risk falling asleep. The latter has the potential for death, but I didn't feel that lucky tonight.

I set my glass of Voodoo on the side of the tub and started dipping my toe in the hot water. I liked it warm, but tonight it was scorching. After tip toeing around the tub, I finally said *screw it* and sat down. Hannah used to take baths all the time, but the tub hadn't been used too often in the last year.

I laid down and let the warmth cover my body. As I dipped my head lower, the water slowly covered up my ears. It muffled any sound, and it began to feel like I was departing my body. I stayed motionless and let my mind wander. I tried to see Hannah and relive the dream when she came to me. Sometimes, if I drank enough, I could start to see her again. With my eyes closed, I slowly moved down further. My eyes and mouth were now under water. Only my nose was left above. When I was in that position, it felt like I was in between this life and the next.

There was about an inch until my nose was underneath the water and I began my journey to the other side. I had put myself in that position a few times, but that last inch was the hardest. My other senses were muted, and only breathing mattered. If I could push myself that last inch, I'd be able to be with Hannah. Even tonight, if I could, I would. I went ahead and gave it a half hearted try anyway.

Our bodies are wired to fight it though. I ended up struggling, and my head popped up. I shook the water off of my face and chuckled.

There was a reason why not many people commit suicide by drowning themselves; it's harder than it looks. Life's little joke: it's easy to drown by accident but hard as hell to hold yourself under.

I wasn't going to kill myself tonight. I knew that even before I went under the water. There were a few things I had to do first. I needed to see Hannah's grave tomorrow and then go back to where it happened one last time. I hadn't been back to Milwaukee, and I felt I should go once before I headed for greener pastures. Once I'd proven that I could go back, then I'd kill myself.

Chapter 2

Detective Owens

The night of June 4th

"If you'll go ahead and finish this paperwork, I'm gonna head home," Eddie said as he slid his chair back under his desk. This wasn't a question; it was only phrased like one. I had gotten used to it.

"No problem," I said and looked back down at my desk. It wasn't that I wanted to do it by myself, but if I could get some peace and quiet without Eddie, then I'd take it.

After my suspension, Eddie remained lead detective. It was Captain's way of continuing to drive the knife in deeper, and it worked. I felt like it was two hundred years ago and I had a large "A" branded on me. If the people who looked at those women were anything like the other cops in my department, it wasn't the look you'd expect. They didn't look at me like a sinner. I didn't feel their gazes pierce me. It was quite the opposite, actually. They looked at me with pity or wouldn't look at me at all. This had a stronger effect than I ever thought it would. Instead of having my anger fueled by their looks, my anger turned to shame. The only anger left was for Eddie and the Captain, and it burned deeper with each passing day.

As Eddie was leaving, I saw him swing his jacket over his shoulder like he was The Fonz, what a schmuck. He wore his jackets a little too tight for an almost thirty-year-old man. He had never fully gotten out of the college phase, and now, even the way he looked pissed me off.

Tonight was an especially busy night at the station. The weather was finally warm, and Friday had the beer flowing all over town. Drinking was normal in Wisconsin, but during the first few days of summer, it can become excessive, even by our standards. The large number of people being arrested meant that we had to start signing people out to clear the drunk tank.

I looked up and saw Officer Bates doing exactly that. She had a large black man at her desk, and he was filling out a personal release form. This meant that for the next twelve hours, he was going to be responsible for whomever she pulled out of the tank. She got up and headed to the back, but I kept watching the man at her desk. He had on an Under Armour sleeveless shirt and tattoos covering his massive arms. I had never seen him but he looked like trouble. He had a permanent *Resting Bitch Face*. He looked like a defensive end with the attitude of a desperate housewife.

Officer Bates came walking in with a skinny white man with a scraggly goatee. The white man had on a black t-shirt with 'Juggalo' from the Insane Clown Posse written on it. The sleeves were cut off, and he had a couple of cheap tattoos on his right shoulder. His face looked familiar, but I couldn't place it at first. Then it hit me.

I opened up every drawer in my desk until I found it. It was the file we had used just about a year ago with Mr. Walker. After my suspension, I put it in my desk, and it hadn't moved since. I searched through it until I found the five pictures of the white guys. They were still in the same order, and I hit the jackpot with the third one. The picture looked a lot like the guy at Officer Bates desk, only plus a couple pounds and minus the goatee. I turned it over, and Justin Jackson was written in the lower left corner.

I looked up to see both men leaving and went over to Officer Bates desk. She was putting the paperwork away that she just filled out. It was a shame that she was such good friends with Eddie because seeing Officer Bates up close, it was undeniable that she was the best looking cop on the force.

"Hey Katrina, what was the guy's name you just released?"

She looked up at me and over to the swinging doors the men just walked through.

"Old case?" She asked.

"Not sure, but do you have his name?" I asked a little more impatiently.

She scanned her paper from the top and started nodding her head, "Yes sir, he goes by Jared Jackson. He lives on the Eastside."

Holy shit! Mr. Walker thought that they might be brothers, and he may have been right. It made a lot of sense that Justin Jackson would have a brother named Jared. Parents have a tendency to name their kids with the same first initial. They think it's cute at first to say little Jimmy and Joe, little Jack and Jill, or in this potential case, little Justin and Jared.

"Thanks, Katrina." I said.

"No problem," she said then smiled, "You gonna tell me why you needed his name, or am I gonna have to guess?"

"I dealt with his brother once and was just making sure I had my ducks in a row. That's all, nothing big," I said returning the smile. "What's his story anyway?"

"I picked him up earlier this evening for disorderly conduct and public intoxication. He was a real smart ass in the car. Asking me if I wanted to slip back there with him and shit. If it was up to me, I would have left him in the tank a long time, but of course tonight..." She gestured toward all the people in the station.

"Gotta love it." I said and we shared a quick smile.

I turned to walk back to my desk and stopped halfway. I went back and felt like an awkward teenage boy for a second.

"Hey, one more thing. What was the guy's name who checked him out?" I asked.

Officer Bates scrolled to the bottom of the same page and said, "It looks like a T. Robinson signed him out."

"Any other information on him?" I asked.

"He wrote down the same address as Jared." She squinted and looked closer, "Never mind, not the same address. Jared lives at 9220 and T. Robinson lives at 9330 on the same street."

"Awesome, what was that street?" I asked.

"Roosevelt, like the presidents," she said.

"Thanks, Katrina." I said and headed back toward my desk.

I sat down and took out a clean piece of paper. I wrote down five names and left several spaces between each one. The first one said *Teenager* followed by *Whitetrash*. By *Whitetrash*, I wrote "Jared Jackson, 9220 Roosevelt". The next name said *Muscles* and it had, "T. Robinson, 9330 Roosevelt" written by it. The last two names said *Woman* and

Leader but nothing beside them. This case had been on my mind for almost a year. I had been pissed off at my partner, boss, and job, and it all centered on that case. The crime dam can only hold for so long, and this son of a bitch was about to break.

Chapter 3

Brian

The morning of June 5th

The sun shone around my folded curtain and brought me back to consciousness. I put my hand up to shield the bright light, but it was too much. I turned my head and wondered why I didn't fix the curtain last night. Once I got to my feet, I noticed that my pants from yesterday were crumpled up and keeping the curtain open. It was at that moment that my head started to pound.

I could feel my heartbeat in my temples, and each throb was getting worse. I sat on my bed with my hands covering my eyes. If a person didn't know better, they might have thought I was praying. If they thought that, they hadn't talked to me in the last year. The last prayer I said in this house was exactly a year ago. I felt no need to sit down and talk to someone who would let that happen to Hannah.

As I stood up, I looked over at our dresser. There was a picture of Hannah and me on our wedding day. She had her hair up in loose curls and was breathtaking. Every husband thinks his bride is stunning, but on that day, Hannah truly was. She was country girl pretty every day, but our wedding day was different. You could feel her presence when she entered the room. For one day, she had all the qualities of a

Princess Diana. I was nervous to speak to her and amazed that she chose me as her partner.

The dresser was in the same condition as it was a year ago. The truth was that the entire house was in the same condition. People talk about how hard it is to throw away deceased relatives' clothes, and they're not lying. Their favorite pair of shoes or pajamas that meant nothing while they were alive were now impossible to part with. Several times throughout this year, I would start going through her things, but couldn't bring myself to remove anything. Her drawers, closet, and toothbrush were all still the way she left them.

One thing that I missed was her smell. The house didn't smell the way it did when Hannah was here. There was no baking smell or scent of candles when I walked into the kitchen. Bubble bath didn't linger in the bathroom. Our sheets had lost the smell of her nightly bath. Occasionally, I would spray her *Juicy Couture* and close my eyes to put me back in a memory. I only had so many sprays left, so I saved them for the good days. If I sprayed it on the bad days, I'd already be out of perfume.

I had one pair of starched pants and one pressed shirt in my closet. Hannah loved when I'd wear blue, so I always made sure that I had a blue shirt in good shape. Most of the time, the way I dressed meant nothing to me, but when I went to her grave, I looked my best.

When I was ready to go, I took two Advil and chased it with vodka. Nothing helps a hangover more than that combination. I could feel the vodka go down my throat and warm my chest. I grabbed the keys to our dually and headed outside. The sky looked about how I felt. Yesterday was sunny and hot, but today was completely different. It was overcast with just a hint of fog. This gave the scenery a grey tinge and the trees a mysterious look. They were hiding their faces from the world. That was how I felt most of the time. I was hiding two things behind my fog of alcohol: my broken heart for Hannah and my hatred for those who had wronged her.

Chapter 4

Detective Owens

The morning of June 5th

Kids were gathering at the corner of Roosevelt and 9th Street near the address I wrote down yesterday. It was 10:30 in the morning, and everyone was making their way to the park. I probably looked like a child molester sitting in my black truck at the end of the block, watching the kids stroll past, but I didn't care about what I looked like today. I was trying to find the missing teenager from my list.

Since I turned thirty years old, every kid in high school looked about the same. The best word I could use to describe them would be obnoxious, but ignorant, helpless, and immature would also be sufficient. This street was surprisingly diverse for being in the black part of town. There was probably some underlying reason, having to do with old jobs in the area, but I wasn't familiar with it. I just knew that there was about a 70/30 ratio of blacks to whites, and that was more equal than most neighboring streets.

I kept a close eye on T. Robinson's address. It was a small, yellow, faded house with a dog chained in the front yard. The rain gutter was broken and hanging off the right side of the porch. The dog was a Rottweiler and hadn't moved yet. Even though he was lying on his belly, he saw every person who walked by. There were three cars in the driveway including the one I was most interested in: a white Nissan. The car matched Ms. Martinez's description before Eddie's bullshit interview muffled her statement.

My phone started chirping, and I looked down to see who it was. The screen said *Eddie,* and I mumbled "shit" under my breath.

"Hello," I forced out.

"Where you at, man?" Eddie started with.

"You didn't get my text?" I said.

"Yeah, I got it. I just wanted to ask you where you left the paperwork from last night," he asked.

"Oh shit, it's on my desk, but I didn't get it done."

There was a pause on the phone. Eddie was probably shocked that he was going to have to do some work today instead of pawning it off on me like normal.

"Oh.. Ok.. yeah, I'll finish it, I guess," Eddie said.

"Sorry, Eddie, something came up last night, and I didn't get to it," I trailed off because I saw the front door of the house swing open. Eddie was getting ready to speak again when I cut him off, "Sorry, I gotta go."

I pushed the *end* button and focused on the people leaving the Robinson's house. There were three people walking towards the parked cars. The first was T. Robinson and his massive arms. This guy never had sleeves on, and I started to think that it was because all of his shirts just ripped anyway. He was the kind of guy that must not ever miss arm day at the gym. The second was a teenage girl. She had on a baggy, loose fitting, low cut t-shirt but no matter how hard she tried, she couldn't hide the fact that she was barely sixteen. The last person was a teenage boy. He had on a baseball cap and zip up sweatshirt. It was the beginning of summer, but some people can never go without their sweatshirts in the morning.

The three of them got into the white Nissan. The teenage boy hopped in the driver's seat while T. Robinson sat shotgun. The girl jumped in the back, and after a couple of cranks, the engine finally turned over. As it started to pull out of the driveway, I sat up and put my truck into *Drive*. I waited for them to turn, and luckily they turned away from me so that I wouldn't have to make a u-turn. At that point, I didn't really have a plan, but I wasn't going to let them out of my sight.

We were both turning on Kennedy Street when it hit me. I leaned over and opened my glove box. Papers flew out of it. I pushed the rest of them to the ground and saw my siren. In all my years as a cop, I had only used my siren one time in my personal truck when I wasn't supposed to. My girlfriend and I were late for the Bucks game, so I did the unthinkable and put my siren on. It was mostly to impress the girl, but I also figured that if I had the thing, I might as well use it.

I cupped it in my hand and started to weigh my options. I could cross a moral line and become a typical piece of shit cop that would pull over a black kid for no reason, or I could justify it and say that I had a damn good reason to pull him over. My head moved side to side as I literally weighed my options. This case had been nothing but blurred lines from the beginning, so I figured "what the hell."

I put the siren on top of my truck and flicked the switch; there was no turning back now. All three people in the car began nervously looking back at me, and I waited for the Nissan to make its move. For a second, I thought they might try to run away, and then their turn signal came on. They eased to the side of the street. When we stopped, I took a deep breath and hoped this wouldn't backfire on me.

I looked down at my phone and shook my head. In today's world, it was never a good idea to approach a vehicle without backup. That was an easy way to end up face down on the pavement. At the very least, you want someone to know that you're about to do so. Unfortunately, I didn't have that luxury today. Technically, I was having a sick day, so I had to fly solo on this stop.

When I got to the driver's side door, the window was still rolled up. I knocked on it, and the teenage kid looked up at me. He couldn't hide his fear, and that actually eased my nerves. We all have a fight or flight response, and when we're placed on the spot, your true colors shine usually through. This kid looked like a deer that was going to run away from the headlights, not run at them. As he rolled his window down, he took a big swallow. "License and registration, please," I said.

The kid pointed at the glove box, and T. Robinson opened it with his right hand. He pulled out the registration and handed it to the kid. I noticed that his left hand, the one I couldn't see because it was nearest the console, never left his side.

"What's the problem, officer?" T. Robinson spoke up.

I looked over at him, and our eyes connected, but I didn't answer. I needed to see this kid's driver's license to get his name, and I wasn't going to do anything until that was in my hand.

The kid handed me his license and registration the way a person hands a baby back to its parents. He didn't know what to do with it, so he just kind of forced it out there, and hoped that I'd take it. I accepted the baby and headed back to my truck.

Devon Robinson was seventeen years old and lived at the same address as T. Robinson. He was five feet eleven inches tall and weighed one hundred and sixty pounds. He must be the brother of T. Robinson because there was no way that the passenger could be his Dad.

I waited a minute and walked the paperwork back to the car. I could hear the voices arguing as I neared the vehicle. I couldn't make out what was being said, but the argument was between the girl in the back and T. Robinson. Like a parent, when I got to the window, the argument stopped.

"Hear you go, Devon Robinson. You have a nice day," I said and straightened to leave.

The kid had a shocked look on his face but couldn't help but smile when he could tell I was serious.

"What the hell you pull us over for?" T. Robinson barked at me.

"Shut up Terrence. He's letting us go," the girl in the back said to him.

They were getting ready to resume their argument when I spoke up. "You have a brake light going in and out. You should get that fixed, but I didn't want to write a ticket for a high school kid," I said and patted the open window frame. "You guys have a good day."

I took two steps when I heard T. Robinson say, "Fucking Pig." I paused, but I knew it wasn't worth it. I still hadn't seen his left hand, and for all I knew, it was resting on a pistol. Devon Robinson might have run from the headlights, but Terrence Robinson wore his fight reflex as proudly as his tattoos on his arms. I had what I wanted, so I walked back to my truck.

The Nissan pulled away, but I stayed parked. I took out my piece of paper and added to it. By the first line that said *Teenager,* I added Devon Robinson, 9330 Roosevelt, and by *Muscles,* I added a note to the end; it simply said Terrence. I would have asked for the girl's ID but she didn't fit the description. She was too young. I now had three out of the five potential suspects, and it was time to do some recon to find the other two. I would have to alternate watching the houses, but sooner or later, the other two would show up. I could feel it.

Chapter 5

Brian

The afternoon of June 5th

Cemeteries in the rural parts of the Midwest were some of the prettiest places you could see anywhere in the United States. They were small, well kept areas surrounded by flowers and trees. They often contained gravestones dating back over a hundred years. Families who had lived in the area could walk around and take a firsthand look at most of their family's genealogy.

Today, the flowers were in bloom, and the trees were slightly moving with the breeze. The grass had been freshly mowed that morning, and the smell of cut grass still hung in the air. The cemetery was empty except for some squirrels chasing each other through the rows of headstones. My family's area was in the Northwest corner, so I had to walk through most the cemetery to get there. I didn't mind. The farther I walked through the rows, the more the world seemed to stay behind me. The sound of any traffic vanished, and I was alone with my thoughts.

As I neared our corner, memories flooded back to me. Wilson Walker was my grandfather, and his tombstone was the first that I saw. He was a man's man. He fought in the army and never lost the edge that places on a person. He was tough on everyone, including himself.

He didn't take any BS from people, but at the same time, he was extremely fair. He had the squarest jaw of anyone that I've ever seen. He started the farm that I now run.

Next to him was my grandmother. Her name was Eva Lynn Walker. She was originally from back East, near Boston, but had met my Grandfather while he was in the service. She moved back to Wisconsin with him. I always loved her accent. She'd say "I love yous" to me, and it would always make me smile. They were married for fifty five years and died eight months apart. Everyone in our town said they couldn't live without each other, and I think they might have been right.

My mother, Francine Walker, was next to her. My mother died when I was nine years old. She was diagnosed with breast cancer, and less than two years later, she passed away. The treatments whittled her down to nothing, and one day I could tell she was going to die. It was in her eyes. When people lose the will to live in their eyes, the pearly gates start to open. Life had been tough on my mother. She had several miscarriages, and it wasn't until later in life that I showed up unexpectedly. I was her only child, but when I think back, she loved as hard as she could while she was here.

My father, Bill Walker, was next to my mother. My dad's name was Bill, not William. That, as much as anything, showed what kind of old school man my grandfather was. My dad grew up in Omro and took over the farm from my grandfather. He had two other brothers, but they moved out West. They wanted nothing to do with agriculture. One was an engineer, and the other sold insurance. I'd only seen my uncles a handful of times in my life. My dad stayed and worked on the farm, so when my grandfather passed away, he inherited everything. My dad carried on the hard working tradition until he passed away from a heart attack about a year after Hannah and I were married. He was checking out the cattle's water tank in the cold part of the spring when it happened. I found him hours later, and he had already passed away. I was an only child, so I now owned and ran our little farm.

The final tombstone belonged to my Hannah. It said "Hannah Walker" and underneath that it said, "Loving Wife and Friend." I dropped to one knee and rubbed the letters of her name. The stone around it was rough, but the letters were so smooth. It reminded me of running my fingers through her hair at night. It was as close as I could get now.

"How are you doing, Babe?" I asked out loud.

Talking to tombstones may be one of the most therapeutic things a person can do. I don't know if there is a heaven, and I sure don't know where it is, but if there is one, I know you feel close to it while you're near a person's grave. The veil between this life and the next must be thin when you're that close to where they rest.

"I know, I've been drinking too much, but I have to. It's the only thing that gets me through the day. I just miss you so damn much," I said.

I continued to rub the letters of her name. I looked over at the empty plot beside Hannah's and began nodding.

"There's something that I have to do, and I don't know if you're going to like it. I know I should try and keep going, but I'm having a hard time seeing the point. I sit around, drink, and think of you. This hole in my heart is just tearing too fast lately."

I put my head down, and tears began to fall inside my sunglasses. I thought that last night's drinking would have helped, but this time it didn't. I had never had to tell her something like this, and no alcohol could soften the upcoming blow.

"Babe," I said through the sobs, "I think that we're going to see each other very soon. I can't go on like this, and if something doesn't change, then I'm going to change it."

These words hurt because I knew Hannah wouldn't approve of them. She would never want me to give up, but she wasn't here, and without her, I couldn't find a reason to live. I might as well pull the plug and see what on the other side.

"I'm going back to Milwaukee to see if any progress has been made on our case. The cops have never called in the past year, but I'm going anyways."

I stayed kneeling in front of Hannah's grave for a long time. When my parents passed away, I cried, but I never took it hard. I knew that part of life was dying, and I could accept that. But the way Hannah was taken from me, I couldn't move on. I had been stuck in a state of depression for an entire year, and I was ready to smile. I hadn't truly smiled in a year. If I ended my life, there were a few potential paths. One of them was that I would go to the other side and see Hannah again and smile. The potential of doing that was worth everything I would give up.

"I love you, Hannah Walker. Where ever you are, just know that I will always love you."

I kissed my fingers and placed them on her name. I stood up and turned to walk away. The thought crossed my mind that this might be the last time I saw this place while still in this life. I could have been kneeling a few feet away from where my body would be resting for eternity. Those thoughts were the kind that pushed a man to drink. I had a long night of drinking ahead of me, and I had to get home so I wouldn't miss it.

Chapter 6

Detective Owens

The night of June 5th

The rain had set in for the evening, but that didn't stop the customers from showing up to 9220 Roosevelt. I was guessing that they were Jared Jackson's customers. Who else would show up every fifteen minutes, stay for about ten minutes, and then slink away? Drug dealers usually thought they were pretty slick when it came to having customers show up at their house. They didn't realize that patterns form everywhere, even if they were trying to have them go unnoticed. A ten-year-old kid who could figure out when the ice cream truck was coming could have figured this pattern out.

The worst part about this stakeout was watching teenage kids walk up to the door one after another. It was one thing to sell to nonworking adults, but it was another to sell to teens waiting to be asked to the prom. Teenagers buying and selling drugs has become a sad fact of life, but it still made me shake my head. If they knew the odds they were stacking against themselves, they'd probably chart another course. Then again, I've learned that people do a lot of stupid shit, no matter what their age, so maybe they wouldn't change anything.

Around ten o'clock the customers stopped coming. I could see that the television was on through the window, but I couldn't make out what was playing. There was no movement for about a half an hour. The night seemed too young for a guy like Jared Jackson to call it quits, and it turned out that I was right. Shortly after ten thirty, a man I recognized walked up his driveway. Terrance Robinson had on a black hoodie, but there was no doubt it was him. He walked more confidently than the teenagers and was the only one to be met at the door by Jared before he knocked. They did the patented slap hands, bro hug, and took a seat on the porch.

The rain had softened and was barely a sprinkle. Wisconsin nights often feel like a green house with the misters on. The rain falls so lightly that you leave your sweatshirt on but somehow cease to get any wetter. The only shitty thing was that the mist made me run my windshield wipers every thirty seconds, and that was not the cover I liked to keep. People might not notice a running vehicle but they rarely miss one with the windshield wipers moving.

I stepped out of my truck and locked the door without honking it. This was pretty bold, but I needed to get a better view, and the only way to do so was on foot. I had on a black and blue, Under Armour hoodie. It wasn't new and wouldn't stick out much in this neighborhood. My gun was tucked in the back of my belt with the sweatshirt covering it. I had on a black hat with little Olympic rings on the side. They had given them out at the office Christmas party after the winter Olympics a couple years ago. I put my hood up and started walking up the street away from the Jackson residence.

When I was far enough away, I turned right and crossed through an empty yard on the same side of the street. I jumped a broken wood fence and started heading back towards the Jackson's house. I was now approaching from the backside. With any luck, the house directly behind the Jacksons' would be empty, and I could get a front row seat without being seen by Jared or Terrance.

My luck wasn't that great because the house behind the Jackson's had lights on but was fairly closed up. The house had a cleaner yard than most other houses on the street. This was most likely the home of an older couple or person. The blinds were all drawn, and I couldn't see anybody through the window. This was going to be a stupid idea, but I had to chance it. I started walking along their fence, heading towards their backyard. Old people were either the least likely to see you or the most likely to shoot you. I was hoping for the first one.

When I came to the last corner, I could hear voices. I peeked around to the back porch, but no one was there. The backyard was empty besides a few toys. Just what I needed, a kid to run around the corner and see me. I looked back towards the Jacksons' house and couldn't believe how close it was to where I was standing. The voices I heard were Jared and Terrance.

For the first time, I could feel myself sweat. I shouldn't have tried to get closer. I was standing in the backyard of a person that most likely had a child and was within speaking distance from two possible murder suspects.

"You gonna tap that?" I could hear Terrance ask Jared.

"Already did," Jared responded, and they cracked up laughing.

I kneeled by the corner of the house and listened. This was my best chance to hear these two and get a better feel for the people they were since they didn't know I was around. The risk of getting caught was something I was going to have to bear for awhile.

The two of them talked about typical guy stuff for nearly twenty minutes. Mostly about girls and what they were going to do with their "real" money now. For some reason, they kept saying the word "real," but I couldn't figure it why. They were either making more money than usual from the drugs or had something else that I didn't know about yet. I kept looking around at the house that I was kneeling by, but there had been no movement since I began squatting. All of a sudden, there were two more voices on the Jackson porch.

"What up, Eric?" Terrance said.

"Damn girl, looking fly," Jared said as he stood up to greet the newcomers.

"You like that?" The girl twirled a white coach purse, "Took it off some high school bitch this morning."

The four of them were standing on the porch, and if I moved, they'd be able to see me. I stayed squatting when I heard something behind me. I slowly looked over my left shoulder and looking me square in the face was a terrified little boy. He was Asian, and his mouth was wide open. I was waiting for a big scream, but he didn't move. He was as frozen as a two-dollar popsicle.

I smiled at him and held my finger up to my lips. I pointed at him and pointed toward the ground. I was hoping that he'd comprehend that I wanted him to kneel with me. The kid might as well have been a dog because he did not understand what I meant. So I took my two fingers, pointed them at my eyes, and then pointed them toward the people on the porch. I hoped that he would understand that I wanted him to watch them with me. He looked at them and nodded his head at me. Then, like a kid late for dinner, he ran back in the house.

I was stuck between looking at the potential murder suspects having a full on reunion a few feet from me and waiting to see if Dennis the Asian Menace was going to tell on me. As I squatted, I started to smell something skunky. Someone had lit a joint nearby.

Once I could see the small puffs of smoke coming above the fence, I raised up to look. The four of them were now sitting on the porch playing a good old game of puff, puff, pass. The girl was taking a hit when the new man named Eric spoke up, "Come on Kendra, pass that shit."

She gave him the joint, and Eric took a long drag off it. Eric had a flat brimmed cap on and a gold chain. The girl, Kendra, had on a low cut, blue shirt with blue jeans. Pretty damn close to the way Brian Walker described them one year ago.

"Good shit, Jared," Eric said as he passed the joint back to the lone white guy. "Better than that shit we used to smoke in high school."

They all started laughing, and their little game continued. About that time, the door behind me opened again. I waited to hear an Asian voice yell at me but there was no sound. I turned my head and the little boy was standing by me with a pair of binoculars stretched out towards me. I'll be damned; this little kid thought I meant I needed to see. I smiled at him and patted him on the shoulder. It was time to get the hell out of here before the wrong person saw me.

As I slithered along the wall, I heard the voices raise, and when I looked, they were embracing each other like they were leaving, too. I hurried by my new friend and turned on the street. I waited to see which direction the couple turned and mirrored them down the street. They were on Roosevelt and I was now on Jackson Street walking the same direction. There were two houses, back to back, in between us, but when there was a space between the houses, I could see them. I tried to keep pace as we walked by house after house until the second to last one on the street. They didn't come out the other side. I waited, but there was no one. I ran down the street and turned the corner towards Roosevelt. I turned again on Roosevelt, and there was no one on the street. The second house from the corner was dark, but as I was looking at it, the light turned on. They must have just walked in. I took out my phone and typed in 9820 Roosevelt.

I walked back to my truck, and no one ever came out of the house. The house was a little run down but in better shape than the Jacksons'. There were two nice cars out front. They looked more like trophies than cars.

I took out my piece of paper and filled it in next to the last two names. Next to *Leader* I wrote "Eric 9820 Roosevelt" and next to *Woman* I wrote "Kendra?" I had pulled two bonehead stunts to get this far, but with a little searching tomorrow, I should have all the parts filled in on my list. The thorn that had sticking in my side was about to get pulled out and it felt good driving home feeling like a cop again.

Chapter 7

Brian

The Morning of June 6th

The sun peeked through the blinds and crept under my eyelids. This might not have been a typical alarm clock, but lately, it was the most effective. I could have closed the blinds at any time during the day, but then I would think, why ruin a good thing? The nights that were filled with Voodoo were often followed by the mornings without an alarm set. Leaving the blinds open was a built in backup plan.

Last night was rough. I don't puke very often, but last night I made the exception. The amount of alcohol I drank wasn't the problem; it was how quickly I drank it. I tried to skip some of the steps in getting drunk, and I paid for it. I was trying to get to the stage where my sorrow drowns before it can take control of my tears. I thought I could grind the gears and keep it to the floor until it stuck. Instead, I ended up resting my head on the cool toilet bowl contemplating whether getting turned inside out would be a good way go or not.

Today, I was going to make the trek back to Milwaukee. It felt like an unholy pilgrimage that I needed to make before I passed through what life I had left. Muslims go to Mecca so they can kneel to Allah.

Christians go to Jerusalem in hopes of seeing Jesus in the tomb. I was heading back to Milwaukee, hoping to feel Hannah in my memories.

I didn't have a pair of jeans left with a proper crease in them, so my cleanest pair would have to do. My white, button up shirt I used to wear to church was still clean. When I made it to the mirror, I couldn't help but laugh. I looked like the messy kid at church. My clothes couldn't cover up the dirty man underneath. The phrase, "can't polish a turd" came to mind. I threw that outfit on the bed and replaced it with my normal jeans and a t-shirt. There wasn't a price on feeling comfortable, but if there was, it would be pretty low today.

My outfit was topped off with my trusty John Deere baseball cap. It wasn't green like every other John Deere hat. It was black with a red outline. I got it for free last summer from a farm supplier, and it was Hannah's favorite. She used to say, "It's original without being original." I didn't care one way or another about it before that night, but now I wear it most of the time.

Our bedroom felt bigger and emptier than normal. At that moment, my life felt like a movie where the camera fades away slowly, except I was very much aware of what was happening. I sat on the bed slightly bent over. I'd planned this trip for weeks, and the thought of finally heading to Milwaukee was literally making my world spin. Anxiety is real, and it was wrapping its warm hands around me.

I inched my way towards the nightstand and fumbled with the mess on top. It was littered with dirty cups and empty Tums bottles. I slid the drawer open and found the buried treasure: a five shot .38 revolver. There is no other feeling like picking up a loaded gun. Danger shoots up your arm like an electric shock. If the book of our life is being written every day, then holding a loaded gun is like wielding the ultimate eraser. Whoever you point the gun at, there is a chance their story ends abruptly.

I held it in my hands like a precious stone, but my eyes went back to the treasure chest. There was a single card in my drawer. I picked it up and looked at the name and number printed on it: *Detective Jack Owens*. I hadn't heard from him since I left the hospital, but I still remembered his name. No news was usually good news, but I had a feeling that no news was no news when it came to Hannah's case. Detective Owens seemed like the kind of guy who would have driven to Omro to inform me if they found the people involved but who wouldn't have wasted a phone call to tell me nothing had changed.

I stood up with the card and slipped it in the front pocket of my jeans. If I was going to drive to Milwaukee, I might as well find out if the case had progressed at all. As I turned to walk out, I noticed the .38 still lying on the bed. The steel was like Aztec gold calling to me. I had no intention of carrying a gun to the city, but as I walked out of the bedroom, I tucked it in the back of my pants.

Chapter 8

Detective Owens

The Morning of June 6th

The office was quiet this morning. At least, I thought it was quiet. I got there early and hadn't said more than "hello" to anyone. I had been so focused on my computer that I missed the morning gossip, but it had been worth it.

My computer skills were weak, but it didn't take an Apple genius to track down Eric Hayes and Kendra Turner. I started with YearBook.com and typed in Milwaukee East High School. Kids from the Roosevelt neighborhood would have gone to that school. I knew Jared Jackson and Terrance Robinson's ages, so I looked them up first. As soon as I was in the 2007 class, their pictures appeared. They each looked like the little kid version of the men I saw last night. I guess we can all say that to an extent, but luckily for me, it rang true this time. Jared Jackson looked like he could have won the "most likely to sell weed" award, and Terrance looked like he was on his way to play football for the Packers. I'm guessing only one of those came true.

The next ten minutes were spent going through pictures trying to match up the name Eric with the face I saw last night. Thank goodness they were all in the same grade, which I correctly guessed they would be, because it didn't take long to find Eric Hayes. Even in a school picture, his cocky demeanor shone through. He looked like every high school kid whose name was Eric, so they grew up loving Eazy E. I'd bet this week's paycheck that he could sing every word in the first verse of the song, "Boyz in the Hood."

The friends we make growing up stay with us forever. We can go years without seeing them and pick up right where we left off. This pack of guys had that feeling last night. A bond was formed in the classroom, at recess, on the bus, and doing every other activity a group of friends does growing up together. That was why I correctly guessed they were in the same grade. The difficult one was Kendra. Women don't have to form that bond over years; they can simply bat their eyes at one of the boys, and the others usually have to accept her.

It turns out she must have been the freshman girl who wanted to date the older guy. I looked through each grade and was almost ready to go to my next resource when Kendra Turner jumped off the screen. She looked like an innocent young girl, someone who might have sold Girl Scout cookies a few years before. She even had her hair in a braid for picture day. The innocence in that picture had long since gone away. She went from a very cute freshman girl to a sophomore dropout. Junior and Senior year pictures were non-existent. If I had to guess, Eric Hayes had a lot to do with that decision.

I took out my folded piece of paper and completed it. Next to *Leader,* I filled in Eric's last name: Hayes. Next to *Woman,* I filled in Kendra's last name: Turner. I wrote "Same" where Kendra's address should have been filled in. I felt like a student who finished a project and knew they had done well. I was looking forward to turning it in to my teacher, who in this case, was Captain Stroup. I kept looking at my list while the last few officers arrived for the day. For a year, these people had walked the streets and trampled my conscience, but with any luck, that would end today.

"How you feeling?" Eddie said as he slung his bag over the back of his chair.

"Good," I answered and then realized he was talking about my absence yesterday. "A lot better this morning."

"That's good; I thought you might have caught the clap," Eddie said in a smartass tone.

I smirked, but my attention was caught by Captain Stroup walking from the locker room towards his office. I stood up to snag him before he was locked in it all morning. I placed my hand on Eddie's shoulder as he rolled his chair forward.

"No clap yet. Your mom doesn't visit until next week," I said and slapped him on the back.

As I walked away, Eddie leaned back in his chair and mimed a dagger going in his heart, "Touche Owens, Touche."

"Hey, Cap," I said before he was able to shut the door. "You got a minute?"

"Sure, come on in Owens," he said holding the door open.

The office was virtually unchanged from a year ago. Every picture was in the same spot as before. His Aaron Rodger's picture still caught my eye before anything else. I had to meet with him a few times after my suspension but this may have been the first time I voluntarily made the trek to his office in the past year.

"What's up?" Captain said as he sat his briefcase on his desk.

I took a deep breath and started to think about how I was going to phrase this. There were parts I was going to have to omit, like everything that happened yesterday, and parts that I'd stress like the fact that these people were most likely murder suspects.

"Well, Sir, you're probably not going to believe this, but I think, through a little luck, I figured out who the people were that killed Mrs. Walker," I said.

Captain Stroup had a bewildered look on his face, and I could tell that I had already lost him.

"The lady that died at the Kwik Stop last year. My suspension," I reminded him.

If a look could say "you've got to be fucking kidding me," then his message was delivered loud and clear. We were both still standing, but I wasn't going to let the awkward pause stop me from delivering my findings.

"Do you remember when Mr. Walker said he thought the white guy could have been his brother? Well, it turns out that the man in the picture was named Justin Jackson, and he does have a brother named Jared, and I believe he was the one we were trying to find. After Jared, I was able to piece together the rest of the gang. I have the completed list right here," I said.

Captain Stroup began shaking his head slowly while looking at his briefcase. He wasn't even looking at me, and I could feel his disbelief.

"This is the real thing, Captain. I believe it. They're a group of friends; we just didn't know where to look. But now we have a chance to make this right," I said.

Captain Stroup raised his hand to signal for me to stop talking.

"Do you have the list?" He asked.

"Yes Sir, it's right here," I said and handed him my folded piece of paper.

The Captain unfolded it and looked it over for a brief moment and then started laughing.

"You really are a piece of work, Owens. *Muscles* dash Terrance Robinson, 9330 Roosevelt. *Muscles*. The description that led your investigation was *Muscles*. Even better, Jared Jackson is *Whitetrash*. And *Whitetrash*'s brother is who sparked this whole thing?" He asked.

"Captain, I know how this looks," I started.

"Just when I thought that there was hope for you, you go and pull this shit. What is with you and this case? Or is it just this time of year?" He asked.

"We didn't do right by them the last time, and this time we can," I said.

The Captain's face scrunched, and his head started to turn the first shade of red. "Don't you start with that goody two shoes bullshit. We did everything within this department's power to find the right attackers. Real cops don't try to hang people based on a "whitetrash" description. This list is nothing but your way to try and think you're helping some country bumpkin couple. You're not; you're just coming close to fucking up five people's lives because they match some vague description from a year ago," he said.

"What about the white car the kid drives? Just like the one the witness saw until Eddie made her think she was incapable of knowing what the color of a car really was," I said.

"Big fucking deal. Google how many white cars there are in Wisconsin. You'll want to arrest half the state. And if that dumbass couldn't remember if it was white or not, then it sounds to me like the good kind of witness to keep off the stand," he said.

"These are the people who" I started to say when the Captain yelled, "Enough! We're done talking about this."

The Captain raised my paper in front of his face and ripped it down the middle.

"I don't want to hear another fucking word about that case ever again. Get out there and do some real police work before I suspend your ass again for wasting this department's time and resources on your own fantasy case," he said.

I felt like a whipped dog. Worse than that, I felt like a whipped dog with a shitty owner, and there was nothing I could do about it. I held my head up as I turned to leave his office. It took every ounce of pride to not let my chin fall to my chest as his door swung shut behind me. I didn't care what he said; those people were the same ones that attacked the Walkers a year ago. I was as sure of that as I was that I would have loved to take a swing at that fat son of a bitch.

Chapter 9

Brian

The Morning of June 6th

The radio was playing Tim McGraw's newest song when I saw the exit for the Kwik Stop. I put my blinker on and eased off the interstate. My chest began to tighten, and I could feel the blood rush up my neck and into my face. If I had worn my collared shirt, I would have loosened the top button.

The Kwik Stop was surprisingly busy for the mid-morning. They tend to be some of the busiest gas stations in Wisconsin, but the night that Hannah and I were there, it was nearly empty. For a year, I thought this was a shitty place that we should have known to avoid. As I pulled into the parking lot, the thought occurred to me that I had been wrong. This was a busy gas station on a typically busy corner. This *should* have been a safe place for us to stop.

I pulled around and watched a white minivan drive away from a parking spot that I immediately took ownership of. I turned my truck off and sat watching the store's door open and close while customers came and went. Most were middle aged women who looked more at their phones than where they were walking. I was a complete stranger, watching them, and they had no idea I was around. Hannah and I had been just like them on that night. I couldn't remember seeing one person on the way into the store. We had held each other and admired the night sky. Could the attackers have been watching us the way I was watching others now?

It wasn't the questions about that night that tore me up inside. It was the lack of answers. Some people draw closer to God in times of questioning. I had not. I found that He often leaves us looking for answers more than anyone else does. While most people ask themselves, "Why am I here?" I had moved on to seek more realistic answers. None bigger than the answer to the simple question: "Why us?" I had concluded through my hours of drinking that it must have been a case of wrong place at the wrong time. But that still didn't answer the question did it. Why us? Why did these people get to leave this same store and go along with their day while ours would never go along again?

I watched a younger couple carrying a car seat walk out of the store. They smiled and could hardly make it to their car without looking down at their baby. This reminded me of Hannah and the hope of a family we once possessed.

I placed my head in my hands and rested my elbows on the steering wheel. I pulled my temples towards my ears in an effort to stop the tears. The lack of answers that emptied my soul was only matched by my hatred of the people that had attacked us. They had not only taken my Hannah; they had taken the thought of children and erased the memories we could have made.

The air was heavy in my truck, and I needed to stretch my legs. I started to walk around when I stopped in my tracks. The pump that our truck had used was vacant. The spot was empty, but images began to fill my eyes that could have been tangible. I saw the woman walk up and say, "Ain't you a pretty bitch?" In a flash, I could see the tattooed man on top of me. I could feel blow after blow connect with my face. I felt the pain from the first hit and the reaction from the rest. I doubled over when I felt the white man insert his knife under my ribs.

It felt like the sun was accelerating towards me and the heat was intensifying. In another flash, I could see the man in the hat hit Hannah in the face and then push her into the concrete block. I don't know if it was the heat from the sun or tears, but I could feel lines of fear dripping down my face. "Black lives matter, Bitch lives don't," the face said to me. I jumped as I felt a hand pull me back to the present day.

"Are you ok?" an old man asked. He had on a VFW hat, and the look on his face told me that he thought I was crazy.

I nodded and finally got out, "Yes sir, bad memories."

"Mmhm, I've had a couple of those," he said. "It's best to bury them while you can, or they might end up burying you," he said and walked away like a god damn Buddha.

I stepped back in my truck and pulled Jack Owens' card out of my pocket. Even though I needed a drink, I wasn't going to try and walk in the store. I looked at his card and thought to myself, of all the people in the world, this might be the one man who could give me some answers. Deep down, I knew he probably couldn't, but for that brief moment, my hope outweighed my pessimism. I unlocked my phone and started to dial his number.

Chapter 10

Detective Owens

The morning of June 6th

When I was in the seventh grade, I asked out the prettiest girl in front of my whole class, and she said no. I had never been more deflated in my life. I had been more pissed off since then, but the feeling of having every ounce of pride ripped from my soul had eluded me. That was until I walked out of the Captain's office one minute ago. He should have kicked me right in the balls and spit in my face. It would have done less damage. I had worked round the clock completing my list, and within two minutes, that fat son of a bitch had shredded it in my face.

I sat in my chair and did nothing. I stared at my keyboard, but it wasn't giving me any answers. I was trying to sort out who was crazy in this scenario. None of my thoughts were completed before another one took its place. Thoughts of remaking my list were sprinkled with images of hurting the Captain. The question of what my job was worth was only preceded by the question of what the fuck was going on?

"You alright, buddy?" Eddie asked.

The chair squeaked as I leaned back and looked at Eddie. I noticeably bit the side of my lip and nodded while linking my hands behind my head. Eddie folded his arms and raised his questioning eyebrow. I always thought he looked like a gay version of The Rock when he did that, but today I actually wanted to hear his opinion, so I indulged him.

"Can I ask you a question, Eddie?" I asked.

"Of course," he said.

I took a deep breath and laid it out there. "If there was an old case that you never solved, and later on you found out who did it, would you go after them?" I asked.

"Fuck yeah," he answered, "I'd go Magnum PI on their ass."

"That's what I think too," I said.

"Did you solve an old case or something?" Eddie asked. "I'm ready to hit the siren if you're ready."

"Not yet. I didn't as much solve it as it kind of fell into my lap. You're not even going to believe me when I tell you this," I said.

"Go on man, I'm getting hard over here," he said.

"Two days ago, I saw a man named Jared Jackson at Katrina's desk. We don't know Jared, but we did see a picture of his brother, Justin Jackson, about a year ago. Do you remember the Walker case? The man that Brian Walker thought looked like could be a brother, was actually the guy's fucking brother. Can you believe it? It was right in front of us the whole time," I said

Eddie leaned back in his chair and soaked up what I told him.

"The son of a bitch is a drug dealer, and I think I found the other four involved. They all live on the same street like a bunch of god damn neighbors from hell," I said.

Eddie kept moving his hands from his mouth and back to the desk. He was visibly thinking, but it had been about ten seconds, and he hadn't said a word yet.

"Shit… the Walker case. Are you sure man?" He asked.

"I know," I said in acknowledgement of the case that derailed me last year. "But this is the real thing. I know it as sure as I'm sitting here."

Eddie kept tapping his foot underneath his desk like a rabbit stuck in neutral.

"Have you told the Captain yet?" Eddie asked.

"What do you think I just did?"

"Well… What'd he have to say?"

I folded my arms across my chest and stared at Eddie. The office was full, and yet no one had any idea how meaningful the next few minutes could be for the Walkers' justice.

"Eddie, for once, I want you to think for yourself and tell me what *you* think we should do. Not the Captain, not the fucking handbook, you as a detective, what do you think we should do?" I asked.

Eddie narrowed his eyes for a few seconds and then shook his head. The poetic bastard even started laughing. His next sentence shouldn't have surprised me, and yet it did.

"As a detective, I'd do what the Captain wants, and I'd follow the fucking handbook. I'm guessing from your answer that he told you to go fly a kite with this theory, so I'm going to kindly ask you to do the same thing. This case is like the crazy bitch a guy can't get over for you. My advice would be the same now as with the crazy bitch: get over her by getting on the next one," Eddie said and turned back toward his desk, ending the conversation.

There were so many things I wanted to say to him, but what was the point? When a person's mind is closed, the only one that can open it is themselves. I started to recreate my list, and again the question came across my mind: what was the point? Defeat was starting to sink in through the cracks when fate showed its face. This time, its face was bright and manifested itself as an incoming call. I usually decline numbers not from the Milwaukee area, but this time I tapped accept "Hello."

Chapter 11

Brian

Lunch time on June 6th

"**D**o you want to order?" The waitress, who smelled like cigarettes, asked in her annoyed but still trying to act pleasant voice.

"Not yet I'm meeting someone here, but I'll take some kind of light beer in the mean time," I said.

She glanced at the clock on the wall and asked, "Busch lite, ok?"

I nodded and looked away. If I was going to drink, I didn't need Flo judging me. I already gave in by ordering a beer rather than my normal Vodka /Mountain Dew. The diner was old and probably wouldn't pass an inspection. There were crumbs on empty tables, and Rush Limbaugh played on the radio behind the counter. The rough waitress knew almost every customer by name. I'm surprised in this throw back dump that she didn't just light up a cigarette to ease her nerves.

The front door hit an overhanging bell which rang as the newest customer entered. I looked up and recognized the man. He hadn't shaved in a couple days, but he still wore a professional look underneath his cheap suit. I wasn't sure if he'd remember me, but when we made eye contact, he nodded and made his way over. The respectful thing might have been to stand up as he arrived, but I settled for gesturing to the other side of the table for him to sit.

"How have you been, Mr. Walker?" He asked.

As Detective Owens finished his question, Flo showed up with my half-cold beer.

"Would you like anything to drink, or are you ready to order?" She interrupted.

"I'll just take water for now," he said.

I tipped my can towards him and said, "How's it look like I'm doing?"

He nodded, "I can't imagine what it's been like. I feel horrible."

"You feel pretty bad, huh?" I took a drink of my beer, "I guess that makes two of us."

The waitress delivered the water but was smart enough to move along before asking any more questions. We sat in silence for a while, but neither one of us minded. We kept looking at each other, me drinking a beer, and him not touching his water. There was a lot being said in those silent moments.

"So, I'm not going to beat around the bush, Detective. I came down here one last time to see if there was any news on my wife's killers. See, they aren't just attackers; she died, so they are killers. But in a year, I haven't heard a word, so is the any news?"

Detective Owens took a deep breath and started to speak but stopped. He picked up his glass of water and sipped it. He was clearly stalling, but I couldn't wait.

"Well, I guess I wasted my time coming down here. I wasted yours too calling you here, should have figured not a damn thing has been done in a year."

"It's not like that," he spoke up. "I'm a helluva lot closer than you think."

I raised my arms slightly above the table with my palms up, "Where are they, then? If you're close, then go get them. Or maybe you're not close and that was just bullshit. I don't have much time left for bullshit. Just shoot me straight," I said.

"I wish it was that easy. I wish that I could stand in front of them knowing that I was the good guy and they were bad guys. I'd shoot them like Wyatt Earp and be done with it. Hell, once in my career, I'd love that scenario, but it's never that easy. There's always bullshit, and in many cases, it's bullshit wrapped in caution tape. Sometimes, I feel like I fight the system as much as I fight the fucking bad guys," he said.

I took a long pull on my beer, finishing it like college kid, and set the empty can on the table.

"Is that what happened a year ago? Did what happen in Cleveland happen in Milwaukee first, but nobody cared enough to report it?" I asked

"I don't know. I can't talk about it," he said.

"You can't talk about it? My wife is dead. Nobody has done a thing about it in a year, and you can't talk about it?"

"Decisions are made at the top. I'm a foot soldier. They send me in the shitstorm, but I don't make the battle plan. You get where I'm coming from?" He asked.

I always thought that Detective Owens looked like a marine, and this little comment just about sealed that thought.

"So, who should I be talking to then? Your Captain? Your pencil necked partner?" I asked.

"Those would be good places to start," Owens said and tightened his fist. "You're more than welcome to, but you're not going to get anywhere with them."

The bell rang in the distance, but I didn't raise my head to the door. We maintained eye contact. Each one of us was pissed, but I doubted many inside the diner would have noticed.

"That's it, huh? Hannah's dead, and everyone just goes on their way like it never happened?" I squeezed my beer can, "Well, it did happen, and I haven't forgotten. There has to be a way to bring her justice," I said.

"We will. I haven't stopped, and like I said, I'm closer than you think. It'll just take time."

I leaned forward. "That's one luxury that I'm running out of."

Detective Owens squinted at me but didn't say a word. He was processing the meaning behind my words, but I didn't care what he thought at this point. One luxury a person did have when he knew he was going to leave this world soon was that the fear of what other people thought vanished.

"You just told me what your wish was. Now let me tell you mine. I wish that I could stand in front of the people that took my Hannah and exact the revenge that they deserve." I paused and nodded, "Besides, revenge is just God's way of completing the circle. But I don't see that happening, so I am going drink until the day I get to see her again," I said.

Detective Owens' phone started chirping like a bird, and he wrestled it out of his pocket. There was a picture of a blonde woman on the screen.

"Do you mind if I answer this real quick?" He asked.

I nodded, and Owens got up and walked away from our table. I gestured the number one over to the waitress and she brought me a second beer.

"Don't go too overboard. It's still a couple minutes before noon yet," she said like a mother.

"This stuff is like water," I said and forced a smile. "I just need enough to get me where I'm going tonight."

Chapter 12

Detective Owens

Noon on June 6th

"Sorry about that. I just needed to make sure that she didn't need something," I said and sat back down at the table.

"Girlfriend?" Mr. Walker asked.

"Sort of. I don't know. She's a pretty girl, but she's only a senior in college. My head was pretty fucked up a year ago, and she helped get me back in the swing of things. I don't know where it will go."

"That was an interesting ringtone for a cop?" He asked.

I laughed, "It only rings like that for her. It's a long story."

Mr. Walker just sat there, and I realized that I'd look like a dick if I didn't tell him the story now.

"My first name is Jack. So as a nickname, she started calling me Sparrow because of Jack Sparrow. One night, she must grabbed my phone and put a bird squawking as the ringtone when she calls. It scared the shit out of me when it went off the first time, but it made her laugh, so I never changed it."

For the first time since I sat down, Mr. Walker actually smiled. The corner of his mouth rose, and a glimmer of happiness showed through. It didn't last long, but it was there.

"If I were you, I'd never change it. It's the little things like that you'll remember if it works out." He continued, "What's her name?"

"Jennifer," I said. "But don't call her Jen or Jenny. Her name is Jennifer, and she'll correct you if you don't use her full name."

"Hannah and I didn't really have nicknames for each other. She was just Hannah, and I was just Brian. But that was ok too," he said.

The talk of Jennifer and now Hannah had softened the feel in the booth. Mr. Walker continued to drink his second beer, but I didn't mind. I had a feeling that it would take a lot more than two to affect him at this point. I'd ask him if he wanted to eat, but I'm pretty sure that these beers were his lunch.

"I miss her every day," he said.

I nodded but was lost for words. This man's pain was sadder than any country song I'd ever heard. He looked like a man on the edge of death and he was willing to jump.

"I know I should have started to heal, or whatever, but it just didn't happen," he said and looked out the window. After a deep sigh he went on, "Sometimes, I wonder if she thinks about me as much as I think about her."

"I'm sure she does. If anything goes over to the other side, I'd think it'd be love," I said.

"I don't know what is on the other side, but I do know one thing: when I cross over, Hannah will be waiting for me in a beautiful field. I'll get to see her and feel her again. That moment is the one thing that I long for every day. And if she isn't there, it will have been worth the risk to get there," he said and pulled out his wallet.

This man basically just told me that he was going to commit suicide. I looked for the words, but I couldn't find them. He was about to end his life, and it was partly my fault. I had done nothing to actually help this man. I found the people he described, but they were still on the streets. I couldn't help but think of my Dad at that time. The last thing he ever told me was, "Do what your heart knows is right."

The silverware was wrapped, so I unrolled it on the table. I took out my pen and thought about what Mr. Walker had said to me a year ago. I wrote down two sentences and folded the napkin. It was only ten words, but I hoped it would help him not pull the trigger. As Mr. Walker was standing up, I handed it to him. He didn't try to hide his confusion.

"If you ever get to the point where the risk is worth it, I'd like you to read what's on this napkin. It's not much, but it might bring you some comfort," I said.

Chapter 13

Brian Walker

The night of June 7th

The last drink in my second bottle of vodka was staring me in the face. I also had the perfect amount of Mountain Dew for one more drink. It was rare that the amount of Vodka and the amount of Mountain Dew ran out at the same time. It was more of a hot dog and hot dog bun relationship. I usually had half a Mountain Dew go to waste, or my night would end with a shot of vodka by itself. I guess fate could see the handwriting on the wall or at least the handwriting on the table.

I had been working on my suicide note most of the evening. Writing a suicide note after a twenty four hour bender wasn't the best planning, but a person works with the hand they were dealt. My first one consisted of two sentences, and basically said that I had killed myself. Even I knew that was subpar work and crumbled it up. The trash was overflowing, so I just threw in over by the rest of the trash on the floor. As I stared at the crumpled note on the floor, I realized that people would think I was a slob, so I took the trash out. My Grandpa used to say, "The first and last impressions are all a person really has."

The second note could have been an N.W.A rap song. I went off on a tangent about the incompetent cops in Milwaukee for most of it and how I hoped the people who were responsible for Hannah's death would rot in hell. I didn't even finish it before I crumpled it up and threw it in the new trash bag. My pen was beginning to fade, so I found the last unused pen in the house. Of course, it had been Hannah's. It said "Omro Elementary School" on the side.

After another Voodoo, I finally penned a suicide note that I could be proud of. It read:

To whom it may concern,

I, Brian Walker, knowingly took my own life. The loss of my beautiful wife, Hannah, had become too much to bear. Please sell my livestock and donate the money to Omro Elementary School in the name of Hannah Walker. I don't care what is done with the rest of my possessions. I only ask that I am buried in the Omro cemetery next to my Hannah.

Sincerely,

Brian Walker

The note may was short but efficient. I felt like I needed to leave something behind. I was sure people would know why I did it, but it was never a bad idea to tell the answer. Motivational speakers tell you to write your goals down. They say they'll become more real and motivate you to achieve them. I think I just became a believer. During the last year, thoughts of killing myself were common, but I never went through with it. Writing this note tonight made it a lot more real. There was not going to be a tomorrow for me, and the strange part was, it didn't bother me.

I felt like I was about to board a ship heading to a new world, and I didn't care how the sea fared along the way. The hole in my heart had stretched the seams to the point where each thread was finally giving out tonight. I turned off all the lights as I headed to the bedroom. I stopped at our bathroom and picked up every towel, the clean ones, the dirty ones, and even the towel I had hanging over the shower curtain to dry.

When I entered our bedroom, I used them to cover the floor on my side of the bed. In the area my body would land, I doubled the towels. I knew there will be a horrible mess, but this should help contain most of the blood. There was no reason to make someone's life harder just because mine was coming to an end.

The drawer opened smoother than usual, and my .38 was waiting for me. It was almost like it knew this time was more serious than the times before. As I gripped it, I felt the handle fit perfectly in my hand. My finger was not on the trigger. I was just holding the handle the way a child might hold his parent's hand crossing the street. I didn't know where I was going, but I knew my pistol would lead me there safely.

I opened the revolver and checked my bullets. All five chambers were filled. I spun the chamber and closed it. It wasn't that I didn't want to know which bullet would be my ending. I didn't want to pity the other four.

I placed the gun at my temple and looked in the mirror across the room. It didn't look right. I opened my mouth and placed the gun in my mouth. I had to turn it sideways to make it feel right. My teeth rested on the barrel, and I could taste stainless steel and Winter Green. It was clean enough to not taste prior shots, but I should have wiped it off first. In that moment, I thought back to a western I saw once. The old cowboy said to never kill yourself by putting the gun in your mouth. He said it could ricochet off a tooth and go out an ear. As ridiculous as that sounds, I figured it wasn't worth chancing. So, I placed the pistol underneath my chin and pointed it up. I pressed hard enough that the bottom of my tongue could feel the pressure from the barrel. This was the way I would do it.

My knees were stiff as I kneeled on the floor. The act of kneeling made the room sway, and I realized that I was still drunk but not drunk enough to affect what was going to happen. I closed my eyes and centered myself. I thought of Hannah and hoped she'd be waiting for me. I tried to picture her in the field, and my eyes filled with tears. Even in this state, my heart overflowed for Hannah. I took a deep breath and heard the click as the hammer locked into place. The slightest pressure on the trigger, and I would be with her. I took a deep breath and to my surprise noticed that my hand wasn't even shaking.

My finger was now on the trigger, and I was ready. Fractions of a second before I pressed down and closed the book on my life, a thought flashed to my mind. Detective Owens had given me a note to read before I did this. It probably wasn't worth the effort to stand back up and read, but the thought stayed with me. I didn't want my last thought to be of a stupid note from a cop, so I eased the gun away from my head and stood up. I walked to my pants that I wore yesterday and took the folded napkin out of the pocket. I sat on the bed and opened it.

The note was short, and I read it three times before I finally understood what it said. I ran my finger under the words as I read them. Tears sprang to my eyes and I placed the gun on the bed. I read the note again. I looked at the gun and over to the scene of towels spread across the floor. This would have been a good ending, but not now.

Ryan Alexander
There was one more thing I had to do before I went to be with Hannah.

Part 3

Chapter 1

2016

Brian

The night of June 5th

My grandpa's old, red Ford rumbled as I sat idling on Roosevelt Street. The lights from the houses were slowly flickering off one by one. Most of the living rooms were still lit up from the televisions, but the bedroom lights were fading fast. The house directly across the street was completely dark already. Headlights came towards me, and behind them, I saw the car I'd been waiting for all night. The white Nissan crept along and slowly started to turn into 9330 Roosevelt. Tonight, the car only contained a driver, and I stepped out of my truck when I saw the brake lights come on.

At 12:30 in the morning, the streets were empty. A person would have had to be looking to see me approach the car. I had on black shoes, black pants, black gloves, a black hoodie, and when I hit the cement on the other side of the street, I pulled my black ski mask over my face. I had practiced staying calm, and it was working. I pulled my trusty .38 out of the back of my pants and took one last look around to see if anyone was watching.

The car door opened, and as the person went to step out I said, "Devon Robinson." As he turned, I held the gun to his head and grabbed his arm. The fear flashed across his face, and I could tell he was frozen. He looked at me like I was the boogeyman.

"Face down," I said firmly and thrust him toward the ground. There was a thud when he hit, followed by squirming. I smashed my knee into his back and kept a hold of his left wrist. This was the closest thing I had ever felt to branding a calf in the spring. Devon's shock was wearing off, and he began to yell.

"Get the hell off me," he snarled.

I cocked the pistol by his head and said, "Another peep and you're dead." He didn't say a word, but for good measure, I pistol whipped him with the barrel. I made sure to hold the hammer so the pistol didn't go off. Immediately after, I reached into my hoodie and grabbed the two items inside: the handcuffs I bought off Ebay and a roll of duct tape.

I slapped the handcuffs on him just like the YouTube tutorial showed and made sure that I erred on them being too tight. Now that he was handcuffed behind his back, I rolled him over and duct taped his mouth shut in one movement. I tore too much off, so it covered his left ear. I picked up the gun and the roll of duct tape, and we began walking toward my car. It was more like I was walking while half dragging Devon. He struggled but was too busy crying to put up much of a fight. I threw him in the backseat on the passenger side. I had placed a second pair of handcuffs there with one end secured to the seat. I clamped the loose end to him so that he was now handcuffed behind his back and those cuffs were secured to the seat. I shut the door and got in the driver's seat. Before I put it in Drive, I looked around to see if anyone was coming. There wasn't anyone on the street, and I couldn't see anyone in any windows. I calmly put it in Drive and drove away like nothing was wrong. When I got to the end of Roosevelt, I took off my ski mask. I turned around to see my captive.

"Hello, Devon, remember me?" I asked.

Devon began sobbing and trying to scream through the duct tape. Only muffled sounds and gasping breaths escaped. I turned the radio up and put on my left turn signal. My heart was pumping, and I wanted to let a Ric Flair, "Woohoo" out but decided against it. It wasn't a feeling of total elation; it was more of a feeling of accomplishment: One down, four to go.

We pulled into my driveway at 2:20 am. Devon was awake but hadn't made a peep in forty-five minutes. I kept looking at him through the rearview mirror, and he was staring back at me. He looked like a lost puppy that just got pulled from the litter. It wasn't anger that filled his eyes the way I expected; it was pure fear at this point.

"That is my house," I said as we passed it. Our blue dually was sitting in the driveway. I wasn't going to drive it on these dangerous trips. There was already bad luck associated with that truck. "That is our main cow barn there, well, it used to be." I pointed to it as we continued on another hundred yards, "But this is your home for a while. My grandpa used to raise mink, and this little brick building is the perfect place for us to get acquainted."

I stopped the truck and went over to Devon's door. He had pulled himself as far away from it as possible, but it was no use. I unlocked the second set of handcuffs and escorted him into the building with my .38 in his back. His tears began to flow again when as we entered. The first room was completely empty.

"As you can see, this building is very simple. This room is 40x40 and was where the cages were kept. There hasn't been a mink in here in twenty-five years, and you can still smell the mink shit." We continued walking toward the next door, "This is where they killed the mink. The stone table is four inches thick. It always reminded me of the one Aslan was killed on."

At that moment, Devon saw the chiseled out corner of the room and coffin placed inside of the hole. He began screaming and pulling away from me.

"Don't worry kid. That's not for you. We all have our parts to play, and that's not yours," I said as I opened the last remaining door. "This room is yours. As you can see, both of these rooms are 20x20, so they're not too cramped. This was where they hung the pelts after they skinned them."

The room had a mattress on the floor in the far left corner with a blanket and pillow on it. There were three different chains coming out of the ground. The rest of the room had various chains hanging from the roof and vices bolted to floor.

"I'm going to chain your wrist, an ankle, and put one around your waist. You'll be able to move around some, but I can't risk you getting away or, worse yet, interfering with what's going to happen in here," I said.

Once he was chained to his new living area, I signaled for him to take off the duct tape. He slowly pulled it off until he realized it was easier to just rip it off.

"Will you please hand me your cell phone?" I asked.

To my astonishment, he handed it to me without a fight.

"Thank you. I'll make sure that you always have water, and I'll bring you food in the morning and at night. The bucket is your bathroom. I'll dump it outside. Do you have any questions?" I asked.

"Why are you doing this?" He asked. "Why'd you pick me?"

"I didn't pick you Devon. You and your friends picked my wife and me two years ago. I'm just here to complete the circle."

"Complete what circle?" He pleaded.

"The circle of revenge. I stopped believing in the Bible for a spell, but I actually agree with some of it. People have been translating the Bible to meet their own needs for years. I decided to do the same. The first lesson you will learn is this: Do unto others as you will have done unto you.

I stood up and started for the door. The chains rustled behind me before I heard his voice. "Are you going to kill me?"

I turned to Devon. "There is a better chance that you will be the death of me than that I kill you. But if you give me no choice, I won't hesitate. Like I said, we all have a part to play. What did you do that night at the Kwik Stop?"

"I don't know. I drove, I guess," he said.

"No, what you did was watch. Since you watched two years ago, then your punishment is to watch again. Only this time, it will be your friends on the receiving end. Good night, Devon. Feel free to yell all you want. No one is going to hear you."

Chapter 2

Detective Owens

The morning of June 6th

"Hey babe, did you move my keys?" I asked as I rustled through the junk on the table.

"Babe, I'm serious. Have you seen…"

"Do you mean these keys?" Jennifer asked with a smile.

She had on a Chicago Blackhawks jersey and nothing else. The jersey was mine, so it went damn near to her knees, but somehow that made it look even better. Her blonde hair was up in a pony tail, and the only makeup she had on was her mascara. It was days like this that it was hard to go to work.

"Thank you. Where'd you find them?" I asked.

"Right where you always leave them, in your pants from yesterday," she said.

"I don't know what I'd do without you," I said and was actually starting to mean it. Jennifer started out as a fling and in two years had developed into someone I couldn't imagine living without. Not to sound like an actor on Bravo, but she actually was making me into a better person. I was more patient at work with Eddie and had learned to bite my tongue with the Captain because of her.

I walked over to get my keys from her and stole a kiss while I was at it. She smelled like Japanese Cherry Blossom, and I had to walk away before things got out of hand.

"Hey, don't be getting in trouble at work now. It's that time of year and I don't want to be getting a phone call from the principal," she said jokingly.

"You don't have to worry about that, babe. Those days are behind me," I paused for a moment and thought of Brian Walker. To my knowledge, he was still alive, but I hadn't heard a word from him since the diner a year ago. I checked with the Omro police department for months after our visit to see if he committed suicide. But when he didn't, like with most things in life, time got away from me, and now I don't know if he was alive. I would have to check into that sometime soon.

I smiled at Jennifer and continued, "Besides, things have been slow at the office lately."

Chapter 3

Brian

The night of June 6th

One high school kid after another came and went from Jared Jackson's house. A few of them may have been older, but they all looked like teens to me. I'd been watching his house for several months, and I would guess that eighty percent of his business was teenagers. How the police hadn't caught on to him was astounding. Jared was arrested about ten months ago, but he only served six weeks for whatever he did.

Once the stream of customers stopped, I prepared myself for what would come next. I wore a ragged pair of jeans, ripped shoes, my black hoodie, and a Brewer's hat. My clothes were wrinkled and dirty so that I'd look like a junkie. My .38 was tucked away in my sock, and my secret weapon was in the pouch of my sweatshirt.

The internet was truly an amazing place. It took me about two minutes to figure out how to make a homemade form of chloroform. All a person needed was the right combination of acetone and hypochlorite bleach. The worst part about it was testing it on myself. The smell could peel the hide off a skunk. I took a rag and a stop watch and timed how long it took me to come back to consciousness. He wouldn't make it back to Omro, but we'd make it out of Milwaukee, and that was good enough. All it had to do was knock him out long enough to get him handcuffed in the truck. I wasn't going to chance it with a grown man the way I did it with Devon.

I could hear rock music blaring at the bottom of his stairs. It sounded like a grudge band concert by the time I made it to his door. I knocked on the door and waited: nothing. The second time, I pounded on the door so that I knew he heard me.

The door cracked open and Jared Jackson peeked out at me. His face was red, and his eyes were bloodshot. The door chain was still hooked. "What the fuck do you want?"

I tried my best to seem fidgety, "Terrance told me come see you if I needed a fix."

"How the fuck do you know, T.?" He asked.

"I met him a couple years ago. Then, a few months ago, we were together in County and he gave me your name. Said you guys were cool. He said you were the man to talk to," I said.

"I don't like people I don't know, but I'll let you slide because of T.," he said and opened the door.

The filth of the house was only covered up by the blaring rock music. "I've got a bullet with your name on it" kept repeating which made it hard to stay focused. We were in what appeared to be the living room. There was a television and a couch, but there were also a bunch of pizza boxes stacked up in the middle of the room. Cigarette butts littered the floor, and a pile of what appeared to be unrolled cigars sat the television.

"What do you need?" He asked. "I've got a little bit of everything, but it's not all high quality."

"You got any meth?" I asked.

"Just the best shit cooked in Illinois. You got any money?"

I pulled my wallet out and handed him everything in it. There was exactly two hundred dollars that I'd pulled out of the ATM on the way here. The bills were crisp which I didn't realize would look bad until now, but if I was lucky, he wouldn't notice.

"Give me whatever this can buy, Man," I said.

Jared chuckled and said, "Not much, wait here."

My hands were in my hoodie pouch, and I was already soaking the rag. As he turned, I pounced. I tried to grab his nose with my left hand and shove the rag down his throat. The music kept blaring, and the fight was on. We hit the wall, and whatever was on it came crashing down. I could hear glass break. I had my right arm in a full choke hold with his throat deep in my elbow. I grasped his torso with my legs and squeezed as we hit the ground. He was on top of me pushing, trying to drive me in the floor, but I was firmly in control. I looked like a WWE wrestler with a sleeper hold on him, and he was now starting to give out. I could feel his body going limp, but I continued to apply pressure. It wasn't until I knew he was out that I released the hold.

The handcuffs fell out of my hoodie and somehow ended up across the floor. I quickly grabbed them and handcuffed him behind his back. He was out, but there was no way to know for how long. At that point, I was just glad that he wasn't dead. He wasn't much use to me in that state. I searched him but didn't find anything but money.

Before we left, I had to find his room. His house somehow got progressively worse the farther I got away from the door. It smelled like a skunk lived with him. I finally came to a room that contained a huge

171

bong on the dresser. But what the bed stand had resting on it was more interesting to me. I put it in my pocket and looked at the mirror. I pulled the red marker from my left pocket and wrote a little message for Detective Eddie Thompson.

There wasn't any good way to get Jared Jackson to my truck. I picked him up and fireman carried him out the door. When I placed him in the backseat, I saw two kids down the street. I secured the two handcuffs together and hurried to the driver's door. The kids were pointing at my truck, and I knew I needed to get the hell out of Dodge. My truck rolled over twice but didn't start.

"Come on, you son of a bitch," I said out loud. Old Red must have heard me because it fired up on the next crank. I drove down Roosevelt at a normal speed and put my left turn signal on. The kids didn't follow, and they didn't run for any houses. That could be a problem, but I would worry about that tomorrow.

We were fifteen minutes down the road when Jared woke up. The first thing he did was throw up on my backseat and then commenced fifteen minutes of nothing but the "F" word.

"What the fuck is going on?" "Who the fuck are you?" "I'm going to fucking kill you" were his three favorite sayings. I never said a word to him the whole trip. At first, I just didn't want to speak until he was done yelling. Then, I realized that not speaking actually bothered him more. After a while, it actually started to amuse me that not speaking was making him angrier. This would make me smile, and he'd get even angrier. "I'm gonna fucking kill you, stop laughing you twisted fuck. Take these cuffs off me and see what happens," he'd say, and I'd just keep smiling.

I pulled up to the mink building and put it in Park. I opened his door and he immediately started kicking at me. He was like a chained dog that couldn't quite reach his target. I took out my homemade chloroform and the rag.

"I'm sorry, Jared. Time to go back to sleep," I said and jumped on him before he could kick me. This time it was much easier than the first. Once he was out, I undid the second pair of handcuffs and carried him into the brick building. When I opened the last door, Devon shielded himself from the light.

"I found you a roommate for the night," I said. "Don't worry. He's alive."

I reached up and grabbed one of the chains. I connected it to his handcuffs. I stepped back, and Jared hung from the ceiling by his hands like a whitetrash piñata. I left the room and brought a chair back with me. I set it behind him and went to the corner. From there, I could lengthen my pulley system out and give him enough slack to sit in the chair. Once the chain was long enough, I placed his limp body in the chair. The last step was fastening the chains around his feet so that they were bolted to the floor. Devon never said a word; he just watched. We were too far away for him to reach us, and I'm sure he knew that.

"Alright, Devon. When Jared here wakes up, you should probably fill him in on what's going on." I slapped Jared on the back, "Tomorrow is gonna be a long day for him."

Chapter 4

Detective Owens

The morning of June 7th

"Would you rather have a million dollars or perfect health your whole life?" Eddie asked as he drove.

"I guess that depends on if I knew I was ever going to get sick," I replied.

"I think I'd take perfect health. It would be great to be able to live your life never having to worry about getting sick. This cold sucks. My eyes water and nose runs like a god damned four-year-olds. It's been four days and isn't getting any better," Eddie whined.

"Yeah, but if you had perfect health, what would you bitch about?" I asked.

We both laughed half heartedly. Jabbing each other was the thing we'd become the best at. It was actually the thing that felt the most like a partnership. I don't like Eddie as a person, but I'd come to tolerate him as a partner. He was a kiss ass, but at least he was there every day. Jennifer always told me that had to be worth something. I guess it's true that if you give someone enough time, you'll find something good about them.

We turned onto Roosevelt Street, and I couldn't help but think of my adventure last year. I was running down the street shadowing that couple like I was on an episode of Blue Bloods. I couldn't remember which house it was, and we didn't go far enough down the street to remind me. The house we were headed to belonged to Sasha Webber. She had a complaint about a strange man last night. We went up and knocked on her door. An older African American woman answered the door.

"Hello ma'am. We're with the police, and we're looking for a Sasha Webber," I said.

"Yes, that's me," she said.

"Perfect. We understand that you filed a complaint this morning."

"Yes, I did. My grandson thought that he saw someone get kidnapped last night. When he told me, I about dropped out of my chair. I called the cops right away," she said.

"Is your grandson here?" Eddie asked.

"No, he's not. He went down to play basketball at the Y."

"Do you have a way that we can get a hold of him, a cell phone maybe? It's just that the details were very vague on the phone. It said 'a man kidnapped another man on Roosevelt Street,' Eddie said.

"I don't let him have a cell phone yet. He's only twelve years old," she said.

Eddie looked at me, and I'm surprised he didn't roll his eyes. We had had back luck with kids lately. They love to stretch details or forget crucial pieces of their story.

"What exactly did he tell you happened last night?" I asked.

"Kevin told me that he and his friend saw a man put another man in the backseat of his truck and then drive off," she said.

"Did the man put up a fight?" Eddie asked.

"No, it didn't sound like it. He just put him in there."

"Did he speed away?" Eddie asked.

"No, he said he just drove away normal," she said. "But the weird thing is who drives a truck on this street? There ain't no other trucks around here. That's when I knew something was wrong," she said confidently.

Eddie and I looked at each other again. I wasn't sure what to think, but this definitely sounded like a bad complaint.

"Right, well we're going to leave you our card, and if you could have Kevin call us when he gets home, we'd appreciate it," Eddie said.

"Thank you for your time ma'am," I said and we walked away.

When we reached her fence when Sasha yelled, "I bet you cops would look a little harder if you heard a white boy went missing in this neighborhood!" Then, she slammed her door for effect.

"Crazy old bitch," Eddie muttered.

The only thing I could think of was that I was glad she wasn't on guard duty when I drove my truck here last year. Old ladies usually see more than surveillance systems. Eddie was pretty quick to dismiss most calls, but I usually held my cards a little longer. This one seemed like bullshit, but if the kid really did see something, he would at least have our card now.

Chapter 5

Brian

The morning of June 7th

The door creaked as it swung open. Devon was in his normal position on the floor, and Jared was sitting in his chair with his eyes shut. As I stepped in the doorway, he lunged in an effort to surprise me. He forgot his feet were bolted to the floor, and he face planted pretty hard. The concrete floor smacked, and his hands were elevated above his head. The chain wasn't long enough to allow him to lie down.

"Good job, Jared. That seems to have worked out for you," I said as I walked around his now wiggling body. "Sorry it's late, Devon. I brought you a couple egg sandwiches today."

I tossed him a paper sack with two Jimmy Dean egg sandwiches in it. Yesterday, I fed him around eight o'clock. Today, it was almost ten. Even though I knew I was in the right, it still took a few more minutes to gain the courage for what needed to be done today. I walked back to the corner to tighten the chain.

"You ready to stand up?" I asked.

"Fuck you, freak. Get these chains off me and see what happens," Jared yelled.

I started to reel him up like a fish until he was on his feet. As I pulled down on the chain, he came up, inch by inch. His arms became straight, and the chain was tight above his head. I grabbed the chair he slept in last night and pulled it in front of him so that I could take a seat.

"Do you remember me, Jared?" I asked.

"Yeah, you and that bitch were the ones we fucked up a while back. I stuck your ass like pig."

"That's true, you did do that. But I don't really care about what you did to me. Do you remember what you did to Hannah?" I asked.

Jared started to laugh, "Yeah, I remember sticking that bitch too. Where is she at anyway, she leave your ass?"

I stood up and looked him in the face. Jared had a scraggly Canadian mustache and a scar under his left nostril. His teeth were stained yellow and only a few years from falling out.

"'I'm gonna get mine', that's what you said. Do you remember that? 'I'm gonna get mine.' Well, I'm not going to get mine, but I am going to get hers. I'm going to do to you what you did to her." I pulled something out of my pocket. "I grabbed this switchblade from beside your bed. I'd be willing to bet that it's the same one you used on Hannah."

Jared's eyes got big, and he tried to back away but was unable to create any distance. He immediately started jabbering on about how he didn't know what he was doing back then.

"Come on, man. It was nothing personal. We just got stupid that night. There's no need to do anything crazy," he pleaded.

"Actually, it's very personal. You see, Hannah died from that attack," I said and used the switchblade to start cutting off his t-shirt.

"O God, man, please. Please God. I didn't mean for that to happen. God damn it, please!" He begged.

"It's funny you bring God up. I'm going to follow his example. I'm serious," I said and finished skinning off his t-shirt. Jared was now bare-chested in front of me. "Do you think I should follow his example?"

"Yes, yes, Jesus is the way. Just don't kill me man."

"I remember going to church growing up. One of the lessons we were taught was that the seeds you sow will be brought back to you a hundredfold. So, what kind of seeds have you sown? You stabbed my beautiful wife when she was unconscious. You sold drugs to high school kids, and I even sat outside your house one night when a girl, no more than fourteen years old, went into your house, and you had sex with her in exchange for weed. Those are the kinds of seeds you've sown. So, like God's unholy instrument, I'm here to complete the circle, and give it back to you a hundredfold," I said.

I looked over at Devon, and he spoke up, "You don't have to do this."

"Somebody has to," I replied and looked back at Jared. "After the one hundredth stab wound, I'll take you back to Milwaukee. If you are alive, I give you my word that I'll drop you off at a hospital. If you are dead, then it won't matter, and I'll drop you off where it's the most useful. Deal?"

"Fuck you," Jared whispered.

"Hannah fought for days to survive. We'll see how much fight you have."

The first blade entered under his ribs where Hannah's was located. He gasped. I pulled it out and inserted it again right below it. The blood trickled on his knife and on my gloves. I worked down his torso on his left side.

"That's ten, time to switch." I stepped to my left and began piercing his right side. After those ten, I moved up to his left pec and then to his right. Jared's jeans were becoming saturated. The front of his pants were no longer the same color. I stepped around behind him and started on his back.

"Half way home, Jared. This would be a good time to start repenting," I said and continued.

The blood was pooling below him. Most of the holes had small trickles of blood flowing out. It was the accumulation that was starting to add up. After number seventy, I started to worry that he might not die, so I made sure to hit an artery in his left arm. The last ten wounds were only done for show. Jared Jackson's head hung limp, and he died, but it was a matter of principal at that point. I stepped back and looked at the broken piñata. Devon's hands covered his face.

"Are you going to be ok?" I asked, but he didn't look up. "I'm going to go get cleaned up. I'll bring you back some dinner before I head out."

"Are you going to kill them all?" Devon asked without looking up.

I thought to myself for a moment, "How they treated Hannah is how they'll be treated."

Chapter 6

Detective Owens

The night of June 7th

Our front door opened, and Jennifer walked in with some grocery bags. She had on her typical gym clothes consisting of leggings, a loose shirt, and a headband. She walked by the dinner table and into the kitchen.

"I brought home a rotisserie chicken. They actually look fresh today," she said.

"Perfect, that sounds good," I said.

She placed the bags on the counter and looked at me sitting alone at the table. I gave her a half smile, but I knew the question was coming.

"Is everything ok?" She asked.

"Fine as wine, babe. I've just been thinking about something all day, or someone, I should say."

"Do you want to talk about it?" She asked.

Before I could give her the usual answer, I surprised myself and said, "Sure." She sat down at the table, and I started to open up more than normal.

"Yesterday, you made the comment about me being good at work. That made me start thinking about Brian Walker. I've never actually told you about him," I said and raised my eyebrows a little. "It was his case that got me in trouble two years ago, well actually, each of the last two summers. Two years ago, Brian and his wife, Hannah, were leaving Milwaukee and got attacked. She ended up dying over a week later," I said.

Jennifer covered her mouth as she heard of her death. She was always filled with empathy, even for people she didn't know. That was one of the many things I had to come to love about her.

"There was some shit at the office, and the long and the short of it is that the attackers were never caught," I said.

"Shit at the office?" She asked.

"Politics, I can't get into it," I said and then continued, "A year ago, we caught a bit of a break in the case, and then it got shut down again: more politics. Brian showed up out of the blue and looked like he was a step away from his own grave. We met, just the two of us, and I thought I'd never see him again. I actually thought nobody would ever see him again," I said, and Jennifer nodded like an attentive child.

"This next part you need to keep to yourself," I said and leaned forward. "I went and arrested each of the people that he suspected were involved. I had to do it on days that Eddie wasn't at work, so it took awhile. I couldn't arrest them on murder charges, but they all had stupid shit I could get them on. One had possession of marijuana, another had an unlicensed firearm. It was all petty, but it got me in the room with them, and I pressed them all as hard as I could on that night. There was only so much I could do. None of them copped to it. But at least I tried."

"At least you did something. That's more than anyone else can say," Jennifer said.

"The problem is that I don't feel like I did anything. I truly believe these people did it, but there's nothing I can do about it. I want to call Brian and see how he's doing, but what the hell am I supposed to say to him? 'Sorry, they're still on the street,'" I said.

"Don't be so hard on yourself. It sounds like you did all that you can do. That's all that anyone can ask for in any situation." She stood up and gave me a hug. "I love you."

I smiled and hugged her back, "You're probably right. I think I'll give him a call. I'll have to find his number." I looked down at my watch and said, "I'll wait until tomorrow, he's probably not even up right now."

Chapter 7

Brian

The night of June 7th

The first summer rain was tapping on my windshield. Old Red's engine was running, but the windshield wipers weren't. I didn't want to stick out anymore than an old, red Ford on Roosevelt Street already did. Some of the items I had in my truck were bad enough to get me in trouble, but Jared Jackson's dead body in the back of the truck was probably enough to get me life in prison. They wouldn't find a fingerprint on him, but they wouldn't have to screw up my plans. The blue tarp stretched across my truck bed was keeping the rain off Jared's body and me from behind bars.

A trashy, blue car pulled up to the Robinson house, and Terrance stepped out. His hood was up, but there was no doubt it was him. Even in a hoodie, he couldn't hide his massive arms. This man was too big to try and take down myself. It was going to take planning and even more luck.

I pulled out Devon's phone and turned it on. I went to his contacts and found the letter "T". He told me that's what Terrance's name was under before I left. It didn't take much coercing when there was a dead body hanging over his shoulder. I pushed Send and waited for him to answer. As soon as I heard his voice, I pushed the gas and started toward destination number two.

"Devon, where you at, Dog?" Terrance asked.

"If you hang up, I will kill Devon. Do you understand?" I asked.

"What the fuck? Who is this?"

"This is the man who has Devon, and his life is now in your hands. If you hang up, he dies. Do you understand?"

"This is some fucked up shit. Who is this?" Terrance demanded.

"I can promise you this is real. Do not hang up. Devon told me to tell you that last year you got him Bulls tickets for Christmas."

"Oh shit. This is fucked up, man. I'm calling the cops."

"To call the cops, you have to hang up. If you hang up, then you killed your own brother. Do you want to do that?" I asked.

"No, man, no. I'm not hanging up. What do you want? You want money?" He asked.

"I want you to walk outside and turn left on Roosevelt. I know it's raining, but do it anyways."

"Ok, man, I'll do it. Don't hurt Devon."

"I promise you that I have no intention of killing Devon, but if you hang up or don't do what I say, I will kill him and send him back to you a piece at a time."

"I'm doing what you say. Don't fucking hurt him," he pleaded.

I took a deep breath and opened the door of my truck. I had about 90 seconds until he arrived.

"Tell me when you're at the stop sign," I said.

"Ok, I'm here now."

"Head across the street to the East Park. Tell me when you see a red truck," I said.

I could see a shadow jogging toward my truck now. This time, my breath quickened as he approached. If this didn't work, I might have to actually kill Terrance, and I didn't want to do that, at least not here.

"I'm about to the truck," he said.

"Go to the back of the truck, and put the tailgate down. Then, look under the tarp," I said and prepared myself.

Terrance was soaked from head to toe. He cautiously let the tailgate down. As he lifted the tarp, I stepped around the corner of the public restroom only about fifteen feet away. The sight of Jared Jackson's carved up body made him numb to anything else around. I could see his body tense up, and he gasped at the dead body, so I took my shot.

In my hand was a dart gun used to tranquilize cattle. The only difference was that this time, I had it loaded with Midozolam, a human sedative. It took a sketchy trip to Chicago and twenty five hundred dollars to get a bottle about two months ago. I had 3mg loaded in each dart. The maximum recommended dose was 2.5mg, but there was no way to know how much he would actually get before ripping the dart out. I aimed at his lower back and pulled the trigger.

It was a perfect hit. He didn't react as fast as I thought he would, so I shot again, but this one ended up in his arm as he turned. Terrance saw where I was standing and rushed toward me. The dart was still in him, but the fight was on. This stuff was not as immediate as I'd hoped. I didn't have time to pull out my real pistol before he tackled me. I held on tight as we hit the ground and pushed the dart in. He got me away from him and tried to hit me in the face. This was a very similar scene to the one two years ago; he was on top of me, trying to hit me.

The result was much different, though. He looked like an action figure whose batteries were about to give out. I pushed him off of me, and the lights were going out for Terrance. I fixed the tarp and pulled my truck as close to him as possible. I pulled, dragged, and grunted Terrance into the backseat. I handcuffed him just like the rest of them and got ready to pull away. This time, I looked in the rearview mirror. "You got lucky tonight," I said to myself.

I pulled out of the park and looked around. The rain may have been the luckiest thing to happen to me tonight. It made the streets empty and eliminated all the people who could have seen that scuffle. There was one more stop I had to make before I headed back to Omro. Jared Jackson needed to help me send a message.

Chapter 8

Detective Owens

The morning of June 8th

I was brushing my teeth when my phone went off. I looked at the screen and declined Eddie's call. He most likely wanted me to pick up donuts, but I was already running late. My phone lit up, and again, it said Eddie. I spit out my toothpaste and answered it with my toothbrush in my mouth.

"Hello," I started with but was cut off.

"Get to my house NOW!" Eddie said.

"You ok?" I asked.

"There's a fucking dead body laying in my driveway. Somebody stabbed the shit out of him. Just get down here fast," he said and hung up.

I was the sixth cop to arrive at Eddie's house. The caution tape was already strung, and a few people were standing outside of it. Eddie looked like he was the victim at the crime scene. He kept walking around scolding the other cops. When he saw me, he quit his conversation with Katrina and walked straight to me.

"This was no coincidence. Some son of a bitch stabbed this guy like a hundred times and left him in my driveway. They even left the freaking murder weapon," he said before I had a chance to speak. "This was a message."

"Do you know who it is?" I asked.

"No, it's some white guy with no shirt. Come look, he's over here," he started to walk to the covered body.

I pulled back the sheet and saw the dead man's face. I couldn't tell if I recognized him or not. He was so cut up from his neck down that some of his skin reminded me of fringe. All of it was pale and stiff. He didn't have the peaceful look that most deceased possessed.

"Where's the murder weapon?" I asked.

Eddie handed me a bag that contained a switchblade knife. I held it up and studied the knife. There was nothing special about it. It didn't look brand new, but there was also no blood on it.

"They probably wiped it clean," I said.

"I'm sending it in right away, and we'll find out. Maybe the dumbass missed the handle," Eddie said and handed the bag to the forensics squad.

"Maybe, but I doubt it," I said.

"Why do you doubt it? We're probably not dealing with a CSI expert," Eddie said mockingly.

"If you took the time to stab someone almost a hundred times and dump him in a detective's driveway, would you forget to wipe the handle?"

"Who do you think did this?" Eddie asked.

"I don't know, probably an old case or someone we arrested a while back. You got any enemies you can think of?"

Eddie's head was down, but he was shaking it, "Nobody that would do this shit."

I looked at the few people gathered around the crime scene. Everyone looked like your typical middle aged, working class neighbors. There were a few kids sitting on their bikes watching, but no one seemed out of the ordinary.

"Do you know all of these people? Or at least recognize them? All the shows say that killer will come back and watch," I said as I laughed. Eddie knew that I hated cop shows because most of them are predictable bullshit.

Eddie looked around at the few people gathered and shook his head again, "No, I know them all. What do we do, Owens?"

Eddie looked at me like I was his big brother. I was supposed to have all the answers even though he was the lead detective.

"I'd start by getting the body and knife processed. Let's figure out who this guy is. We can go back to the office and see if any of the people we've locked up have been released recently. This looks like something a convict might do to stick it to you," I said.

"I agree, let's do that. We're going to bust this son of a bitch and I'm gonna love doing it," He said.

I headed back to my truck and tried to think of who the dead man looked like. I couldn't place him at the moment, but I knew that I'd seen him before. It's hard to recognize anyone in that state, but it would come to me. In my mind this was one of two scenarios. It was either completely random that this man ended up in Eddie's driveway, or more probable, this dead body was a message to Eddie. The real question then was: Who would be willing to send that kind of message?

Chapter 9

Brian

The morning of June 8th

"Good morning, Terrance. Or should I call you T.?" I asked him while he struggled with the chains. "You're not going to break them, but you're welcome to keep trying. I'd hate for you to lose hope so soon."

Terrance was chained to the same chair that Jared had been in the night before. The chair looked smaller with him in it. The roomed smelled like a slaughter house after Jared bled out yesterday. I mopped the floor before I left, but it didn't cure the smell. I almost felt bad for Devon, but he wouldn't have to tolerate it for long.

"I love the smell of napalm in the morning," I said as a joke to myself. Terrance looked at me like I was crazy. He probably thought I was, but he would have some time to change his mind before he left the mink building.

"Do you know why you're here?" I asked.

Terrance kept his head down but started to speak, "Devon told me that your wife died after that night. I'm sorry. I'm so sorry. Please let Devon go. Kill me, just let him go. He's only in high school."

His tone was completely different than I expected. Maybe there was hope for Terrance after all. My punishment couldn't have been better.

"I'm not planning on killing Devon. You can rest assured of that. I appreciate you saying you're sorry. I really do. It's a little late, but that's all right. You saw what I did to Jared Jackson under the tarp. Do you know why I did it?" I asked.

"Devon said that because he stabbed your wife, you stabbed him one hundred times."

"That's correct. What did you do to my wife that night?" I asked.

Terrance looked up at me with a puzzled expression. "I don't know. I don't remember. I don't think I did anything to her that night," he said.

"Ding, ding. That is correct. You didn't do anything to her. At least, not that I could remember. I remember you beating me, but today isn't about me. You didn't do anything to her."

Terrance looked over at Devon and their eyes connected. In that moment, they shared a glimmer of hope.

"But that doesn't mean you haven't done anything bad in your life," I said, and he looked back to me. "The word on the street is that you killed a man outside a pizza shop when you were just out of high school. Beat him to death is what everyone told me. Is that true?"

I paid two teenage kids one hundred dollars apiece for any useful information about Terrance. The story they told me was more of an urban legend for the younger generation, but I had a feeling there was some truth in it. Terrance hung his head, and in a voice barely audible said, "That was a long time ago."

"What do you think, Devon? Let's keep with our church theme. Should we kill Terrance's brother to atone for his sins?" I asked.

"No, leave him out of this!" Terrance yelled.

"Or should we give him a chance to rise a better man, a baptism of sorts?" I said and continued to look at Devon. He didn't flinch.

"You didn't touch Hannah, but your actions led to her lying in a bed unable to live or die. So your punishment will be the same." I stood up and opened the door so that he could see the coffin in the corner of the other room. "You didn't touch her, so I won't touch you. But, you will get to feel the mental pain that she went through lying in that hospital bed. Then at the end of it, you will get to rise a new man. Sounds damn near perfect, doesn't it?"

"Please don't put me in that coffin. Please don't. I'm sorry," Terrance pleaded.

I pulled out my homemade chloroform and a rag. I began to soak it. Devon was screaming, and in the little room, it was beginning to feel hectic. I walked behind Terrance and put the rag to his mouth. He tensed but was unable to put up much of a fight. Devon lunged at me like a chained dog but wasn't getting anywhere with his efforts. Once Terrance was out, I looked at Devon. Tears ran down his face. "Please don't kill my brother," he said.

"Don't worry; I put enough water in the coffin to last a few days. There are three, one inch pipes that will supply him with enough air to breathe. If he wants to live as badly as Hannah did, he should make it easy. If he gives up, then he should have fought harder," I said.

Chapter 10

Detective Owens

The afternoon of June 8th

Eddie and I were at the office shuffling through old cases trying to find someone who had been recently released. There were a few light offenders, but no one stuck out that would commit that kind of violence. Eddie's phone rang, and he snatched it up. I could only hear his side of the conversation, but I could tell he was getting the info he wanted.

"Yeah, I got a pen. Go on," he said as he wrote on his yellow note pad. "I know exactly where that is. We're headed there now."

He hung up and looked at me, "Fucking Roosevelt Street. Let's go," he grabbed his notepad and strutted to the door.

"What was the victim's name?" I asked as I sat in his passenger seat.

Eddie pointed toward the notepad on the dash, "It's written on there with his address."

He just wrote it down two minutes ago and couldn't remember it. What a dumbass. I leaned forward and picked up the yellow pad. I nearly dropped it when I read the name: Jared Jackson, 9220 Roosevelt. I had to compose myself so that Eddie didn't notice. I pulled the seat belt away from my chest and took a deep breath.

"What was his name?" Eddie asked.

"Jared Jackson," I replied.

"Does that ring any bells?" he asked.

I looked at Eddie and contemplated my answer. I knew exactly who Jared Jackson on Roosevelt Street was, but I didn't know if it was time to play that card yet. When Eddie looked at me, I shook my head, "No, I don't think so," I said.

I thought back to dead body, and sure as shit, that was the man I saw a year ago outside of his house. I didn't recognize him this morning because of the blood loss, and quite honestly, why would it have been him? Now, the answer seemed pretty logical. Brian Walker must have found him and left him in Eddie's driveway to let us know that he found him.

We jumped out of Eddie's car in front of Jared's house and walked up to the front door. We knocked and no one obviously answered. I looked at Eddie, and he turned his back towards me and the door. I tried the door handle, and to my surprise, it was unlocked.

"Would you look at that. His door was left open," I said to Eddie.

"Seems like enough probable cause to enter," Eddie said and walked through the front door.

Jared Jackson was not a clean person. His house smelled like a back alley. By the looks of it, I'd guess they were filled with the same things: old trash, drugs, and cheap sex. Eddie stepped on some glass, and we looked at the cause. One of the few pictures had fallen from the wall and broken.

"This place is a shithole, but I'd guess this is where an altercation took place recently," I said.

"You're probably right, but it's hard to tell in here," Eddie replied.

We continued through the house. The smell of marijuana got stronger as we walked deeper into the house. The bathroom would have condemned most restaurants. There was zero chance it had been cleaned in over a year. The mirror was shattered, and some of it was completely missing. I looked in the tub, and hair was visibly sticking out of the drain. To be honest, I was surprised there wasn't shit in the toilet.

When we reached the last bedroom, Eddie stopped in his tracks. There was a message written in red on the mirror. I stepped around Eddie and read it. "A blind eye for a blind eye" filled the entire mirror.

"What does it mean?" Eddie asked.

"I don't know." I answered, "But we better figure it out. It damn sure means something, or whoever did this wouldn't have left it."

"You think it was them or Jared who left it?" He asked.

"I'll bet my paycheck that it was whoever did this. Call it a detective's intuition," I said and left the room.

I had to get outside and get some air. More cops were arriving as I left the house. Eddie spoke to them and then met me at the fence line.

"I need to make a call real quick," I said, "You should run up and talk with that old lady again. Her grandson really might have seen who did this, and we should get a hold of him ASAP."

"Damn, that's true," Eddie said and slapped the fence. "Who do you have to call?"

"I just have to call Jennifer really quick. You can take the car; I'll walk up there if you're not done."

Eddie stood there looking at me, holding the fence. He wiped his runny nose on his shirt. With all the action today, I almost forgot that

Eddie was sick. I knew what I said sounded like bullshit, but I needed to make a call, and I had to be alone.

"It's important, man," I said.

Eddie nodded and walked toward his car. He wiped his eyes with his other shirt sleeve. He might not have wanted to go, but at least he did. I pulled out my cell phone and piece of paper that I had found last night. It contained Brian Walker's phone number. I had planned on calling him today but not for this reason. Now, he was our number one murder suspect, and I needed to talk to him before anyone else figured it out.

Chapter 11

Brian

The afternoon of June 8th

I patted the dirt that covered Terrance's temporary coffin with my shovel. There were three, one inch pipes that came up through the sand. They connected to the coffin and hopefully provided him with air. I tried it out, but there was no way to simulate it being under about two and a half feet of dirt. If I would have dug the hole any deeper, the hole would have filled with water. I couldn't risk that, so I reinforced the coffin and made do with what I had to work with. There was no way Terrance could have escaped from that coffin even if it was above ground now. I buried it for effect more than anything.

I stuck the shovel in the dirt and wiped the sweat from my forehead. I headed back up to my house to take a shower. The sun beat down on me, and some water sounded nice. A cold Voodoo sounded better, but yesterday was my one year sober anniversary. The day I almost killed myself was the day I quit drinking. I went through withdrawals, but I stuck it out. A new goal consumed my life. I only had a few days left before my task was complete, so there was no reason to start over now.

My phone rang as I entered the house. This had become so rare that it startled me. I looked at the caller ID and saw it was a Milwaukee number. I hesitated but went ahead and answered it.

"Hello," I said.

"Hi, is this Brian Walker?" a familiar voice asked.

"It is. Who is this?"

"This is Detective Owens. How are you?" He asked.

"I'm doing great detective. How are you?" I asked. It didn't take him long to put the pieces together. I always knew he was a good cop.

"Well, I've been better. Work has been getting crazy here lately. Things from the past keep popping up in places you wouldn't believe," he said in a way to make sure I knew that he knew.

"You gotta stop living in the past, Detective. I found a way to bury mine," I said with a smile.

"Brian, I can't talk long, so I'm not going to fuck around. I know what's going on. I want you to know that regardless of my personal feelings towards this situation, I'm still a cop. If the evidence is there, I'm coming after you," he said.

"I wouldn't feel the same about you if you didn't. But I don't think you have to worry about me. I'm just a country boy from Omro. I wouldn't stand a chance against someone like Detective Thompson." I paused, "How is he, anyways?"

"He's sick, so you're going to have to deal with me," he said.

"I'm sorry to hear that. I hope that whatever is popping up down there isn't hurting his stomach," I said sarcastically.

"He's not sick like that; he just has a runny nose and watery eyes. He's plenty well enough to catch a dumb country boy if he has to."

"Good to hear. Well, thanks for the call, Detective. I'm glad we're on the same page now, but you can rest easy. I'm sober, and I've started believing in God again, well, as much as I can. Meeting with you helped me get to this point, so while I have you on the phone, I want to thank you. Thank you for your note. It helped me to not pull the trigger."

"I'm glad to hear that. I really am, but the note wasn't meant to have this effect," he said.

"Love has a different effect on everyone. Have you ever been in love, Detective Owens?"

"What's that have to do with anything?" He asked.

"If I recall correctly, you had a pretty blonde girl you were dating last year. Is she still around?" I asked.

"I don't have time for this bullshit," he said.

I laughed on the phone. Detective Owens seemed so serious all the time, but I think I may have touched a nerve with that one.

"That's fine. Goodbye, Jack, I'll talk to you soon," I said and hung up.

I'd always felt a kinship to Detective Owens. He's the only one that I thought was on my side the whole time. Even now that we were pitted against each other, I didn't feel ill towards him. The worst part about him was that he actually was a good detective. If I gave him too much time, he'd end up at my doorstep. I was going to have to move my time frame up now. I'd have to make another trip into Milwaukee to finish off the power couple tonight. I'd have to stop by the superstore on the way too. Detective Thompson might need something for that cold.

Chapter 12

Detective Owens

The night of June 8th

The center of this case revolved around Roosevelt Street. That was why I was sitting in my truck, eating dinner, watching houses on Roosevelt Street. I couldn't tell Eddie that I knew who was next on the hit list, so I was alone. I was on the same street, in the same truck, watching the same houses that I had a year ago. And yet, everything seemed different now.

I kept thinking about Brian's and my short conversation. He might want me to think that he was just some dumb country boy, but I knew better. The coroner confirmed there were exactly one hundred stab wounds in Jared Jackson. That took commitment and discipline. He didn't just pick him up, kill him, and drop him off. He had to have taken him somewhere where he had privacy and time. My first thought was that he had taken him to Omro, but that wasn't a short drive. This guy would be on another level if he took each of them back to his house and then brought them back. It was more likely that he had some kind of place rented near Milwaukee that he could take them.

I picked my phone up and called the station. Gavin was one of our techs, and we were starting to be friends. I bet I could get him to do me a solid and look up Brian's credit history to see if there were any recent purchases near Milwaukee. The more I could narrow down where he was, the faster I could catch him if he kept killing his attackers.

"Hey Gavin, how's it going?" I asked as he picked up.

"Jack, what's up, man? Are you still out this late?" he asked.

"Oh yeah, I'm on a stakeout tonight. Have you left the station yet?" I asked.

"Yeah, I'm home already. What's up? Do you need something?"

"I do, actually. Do you think that first thing in the morning you could look something up for me?" I asked.

"Sure, I should have time in the morning. What is it?"

"I need you to look up a credit history on Brian Walker. I'm looking for properties or rentals near Milwaukee. Also, just any unusual activity, if there is any," I said.

"I thought you were going to give me something hard. I'll get you that first thing in the morning," he said.

"Thanks Gavin, I'll owe you one," I said.

"Don't worry about it. Have a good stakeout. I'll talk to you in the morning," he said and hung up.

There was no movement at the Robinson house. The white Nissan was out front, but only the kitchen light was on. It had been on the whole time, but none of the other lights had changed. My guess was that someone left it on and that no one was home. Eric Hayes' house was the opposite. He and Kendra Turner were both home, and all of their lights were on. The couple got home shortly after I arrived and looked to be settled in for the night.

My phone lit up, and I answered it. "What's up, Eddie?"

"Can you come to the station tonight?" He asked.

"What's going on?" I asked.

"Kevin Hale, Sasha Webber's grandson, will be at the station in twenty minutes. I finally got ahold of him and his grandma is bringing him down tonight. I told her it was urgent," he said.

This kid could have seen what vehicle Brian was driving, and that would help me out greatly. I needed to get there so Eddie didn't screw this one up too.

"I'm on my way. Wait for me to start the interview; I want to hear what this kid has to say," I said and put my truck in Drive.

"Will do," Eddie said and hung up.

As I pulled away, I looked at all of the cars parked on the street. None of the vehicles appeared to be running. There was a white, single cab truck parked close to the Robinson's house. I slowed down and stared at the license plate. Just then, I passed an old red truck. I didn't get my head turned fast enough to see the driver. I probably shouldn't be jumpy about the vehicles. If I remembered right, Brian drove a blue dually two years ago. Why would he be driving around in an old red truck? I put my foot to the floor and headed to the station.

Chapter 13

Brian

The night of June 8th

I turned onto Roosevelt Street and passed a black truck. I might have been nervous after our conversation, but it almost looked like Detective Owens was driving it. I didn't change my speed, but I did watch him in my rearview mirror. The black truck turned and sped away; it must not have been him. I pulled over in front of Eric Hayes' house and took a deep breath. I needed to calm my nerves. If I was driving around thinking that other drivers were Detective Owens, I'd better clear my head before I made my boldest move yet.

My plan had been to watch this couple for a couple days and then find the right moment to get them both at once. Now, I was going to break in and get them both or one at a time, whichever came first. In the past few weeks, I'd watched the house many times, and learned their habits. It was still different when I was about to cross the threshold. The wonder replaced what my eyes have seen.

The black gear I'd worn every night felt like a uniform, and I was ready for work. My pouch was filled with two pairs of handcuffs and a new toy. A month ago, I paid cash for a brand new taser in Madison. I had waited to use it because I had never tried to get two of them at once. This was the easiest way to incapacitate one of them quickly. In my hands, I carried a hammer and duct tape. My trusty .38 was tucked in the back of my pants.

Quietly, I walked around the house to the back corner room. It must have been a guest room because the light was never on. They were always in the kitchen, the living room, or upstairs. I made a test run a few weeks ago, but all I could see was that the room looked like a mess. As I approached, a dog started barking. I froze in my tracks until I remembered they didn't have a dog. I knelt down and hurried to the window.

It was very humid because of last night's rain, and I was already sweating. When the dog stopped barking, I began duct taping the entire window that I was going to break. I kept looking over my shoulders to make sure no one was looking at me. Eventually, there wasn't any glass that could be seen. Now that it was covered, I tapped the window with the hammer. I thought for sure they heard it, but no one came. After a few taps, nothing happened, and I realized I wasn't hitting it hard enough. Finally, I hit the bottom left corner hard enough to break the glass. Some of it fell into the house, but most of it was stuck to the duct tape. I peeled it back towards me and felt the sheet continue to break off in pieces. When the hole was big enough for my hand to fit in, I unlatched the window and wiggled my way in.

My taser was out, but I couldn't hear anyone coming. I army crawled over to the door and looked around the corner. I felt like a five year old who was checking to see if his parents were still up. The lights were on, but no one was down stairs. I took a deep breath and stood up. If I got caught, I wouldn't be down on my knees.

I followed my taser up the stairs like a cop would, sweeping the house. At the top of the stairs, I could hear a thumping. I listened and heard a woman's voice. I couldn't make out words, only sounds. The rhythmic thumping continued, and I realized what they were doing. It now made sense that no one came down stairs when the window broke. I rounded the corner at the stairs and looked in the cracked door.

Kendra was on top of Eric facing the wall. She was as naked as the day she came into the world. I stood in the doorway watching her roll her hips. Eric had his hand around Kendra's throat. In this incredibly erotic moment, my thoughts couldn't be farther from sexual. They unknowingly had given me the perfect window to seize them with little resistance. I stood in the shadows watching this couple embrace for possibly the last time. They finished, but before I entered the room, Kendra announced, "I'm getting in the shower."

I stepped back in the shadows and waited for her to enter the bathroom. I could smell her cheap perfume, and she never even knew I was there. Their master bathroom door closed behind her. Eric laid on the bed, not moving. His pants were still down, and he was staring at the roof. I was ready to strike.

The door opened without a sound, and I walked directly up to Eric with the taser. I stopped on his side of the bed and waited for him to open his eyes. When he did, it took him a second to comprehend what was happening. The shower sprayed in the other room. Before Eric could speak, I shot the taser into him. As the bolts of electricity hit him, his body spasmed. He looked like he was having a seizure.

I let the bolts hit him until he finally pissed on the bed. I roughly removed the hooks and handcuffed his hands behind his back. Once he was handcuffed, I pulled his pants up and buttoned them. I didn't want to look at a naked guy all night. I picked Eric up and carried him into the hallway. I could hear the water stop in the bathroom.

"Will you go get my phone? I left it in the kitchen," Kendra said. I didn't make a sound while I waited by the door. I could hear the blow-dryer start. I thought of the many times I heard Hannah do the exact same thing in our house. That thought was replaced with the realization of not seeing her do it again because of these people.

The door opened, and Kendra walked out in skimpy shorts and a t-shirt. "Mother Fucker, I asked you to" she got out before I grabbed her around the waist and threw her to the ground. She kicked and threw punches in every direction. I put my knee in her back, but she continued to fight. Her left wrist ripped away from me, and she flipped over. Kendra screamed and tried clawing at my face. I couldn't risk being heard, so I put my hand over her mouth. The bitch bit my hand like an angry pit bull.

She punched me in the face, but I was able to grab her right wrist. Rather than continue to fight on her terms, I took both my hands and broke her wrist. She screamed as her eyes rolled back in her head. I slapped the handcuffs on that wrist and rolled her over. She continued to squirm on her stomach. I put my knee in the back of her neck and grabbed her left arm. Once the cuffs were secure, I stepped back. Kendra was the last member of the group to be captured, the only woman, and yet she fought harder than all the men combined.

I pulled the duct tape out of my pouch and stopped her screaming. The fury in her eyes was barely contained. I squatted in front of her and locked eyes.

"I'm sorry about your wrist; it wasn't my intention to hurt you here," I said and she responded with a muffled but recognizable, "Fuck you."

"Take some deep breaths. It'll help," I said and walked back into the hallway.

Eric looked up at me as I walked past him. I stopped, grabbed his feet, and proceeded down the stairs. He clunked all the way down. I made sure to go down them faster than normal. His attempted swearing at the top of the stairs became only grunts by the bottom. Once we finished, I smiled smugly at him and headed out the garage door.

I started his Camaro while the garage door opened. The car smelled like weed and cheeseburgers. I backed up and stopped in the first available open spot on the street. I grabbed the garage door opener but left the car unlocked with the keys in the ignition. Somebody on that street was going to have an early Christmas. I retrieved Old Red and backed it into the empty garage. The garage door rolled down, and I had the privacy I needed to load the bodies.

First up was Eric. He was functioning by now, so I pistol whipped him once for good measure. I dragged him out and threw him in the back of the truck. Once his hands and feet were fastened to the sides, I tightened the tarp over him. The tailgate shut and passenger one was ready.

I went back up the stairs to find Kendra running around their room. She was trying to get their gun from under their bed, but luckily a broken wrist and handcuffs behind her back made that impossible. She jumped on the bed trying to get away, but I grabbed the handcuff chain and dragged her out of the room. Outside, I spun her around.

"Be a good girl, and you'll get through this," I said.

She shouted again and tried to head butt me. I grabbed her wrist and twisted it again until tears filled her eyes and her knees buckled.

"You're doing this to yourself," I said.

We started to walk down the stairs, and she was more cooperative now. That was until we went into the garage and she saw my truck instead of their car. Kendra started fighting again, but this time, I just kept going and muscled her into the truck. She tried to go for the other back door, but despite her efforts, she still ended up handcuffed to the seat. The duct tape stretched out, and I placed it across her eyes. I knew that would hurt getting off, but I couldn't have her fighting the whole time to Omro.

I pulled out of their garage and closed the door behind me like I owned the place. I didn't feel like cheering tonight. I was all business. The last two were captured and their fates awaited them tomorrow. My only hope was that I wouldn't run into the real Detective Owens before it was done.

Chapter 14

Detective Owens

The night of June 8th

K evin Hale walked in with his pants below his ass and his grandma at his side. He fit every preteen stereotype that I could think of. I hated interviewing kids this age. They were generally dumber than a box of shit. They either acted like they're too cool to talk to you, they don't speak at all, or they speak in sentences littered with "like" and "um".

"Hello, I'm Detective Owens," I said and stretched my hand out. The little bastard looked at it and didn't shake it. He didn't say anything; he just stood there staring me down. I pulled my hand back and said, "Right this way."

I looked at Eddie, and he was biting his lip trying not to laugh. We turned into the first open conference room. Eddie and I walked to the far side of the table and sat down. In this room, Kevin's nerves were almost tangible.

Eddie started, "Kevin, can you tell us exactly what you saw last night?"

Kevin looked at his grandma. She placed her hand on his arm.

"He's not in trouble, right? We spoke up trying to do the right thing, not get in trouble for it," she said.

"Your grandson is not in any trouble. We are just trying to connect the dots, and Kevin can help us do that," I said.

She nodded at him, and he looked back towards us. "Michael and I were out and saw some dude kidnap another guy. He had him on his shoulders and put him in the back seat. That's all," he said and looked back at his grandma.

"Do you remember what time it was when you saw them?" Eddie asked.

He shook his head, "My curfew is midnight, so it was before then."

"Do you remember anything specifically about the man who was carrying the other man? Was he tall? Skinny? Fat? White? Black? Bald? Anything you can remember would help," Eddie said.

"Um, well, he was white, but he was dressed in black. He just looked normal. I don't know," Kevin said nervously.

"Ok, good. That helps us. The more details the better," Eddie said.

"What color was the truck?" I asked.

Kevin looked over to me, "It was a red truck."

"Was it older or newer?" I asked.

"I don't know. I'd guess older. I just know it was red," he said.

I thought back on the night. I passed the son of a bitch coming here. Adrenaline shot through my body. He was going to get Eric and Kendra, and I passed the son of a bitch on his way. We needed to end this; Brian Walker could still be in that house.

"Thank you for your time. This really did help us out," I said and shook Sasha Webber's hand.

They left the room, and I looked at Eddie and said, "We know he's white and drives a red truck. That's a good start."

"Damn straight. We'll start looking for that description in the morning," Eddie said as he pulled his keys out of his pocket.

"Sleep with one eye open. You might end up with one on your roof tonight," I said jokingly.

"I'll blow his ass away like Santa if he tries," Eddie said.

My truck was going seventy-five when I turned on Roosevelt Street. I sped up to Eric Hayes' house, but there was no red truck. All the lights were on in the house. Everything looked the same as it had when I left. I drove down and checked the Robinson's, no change there either. I went back up the street to the Hayes' house. It felt like the one he'd hit next.

I sat in my truck for fifteen minutes before I finally said "Fuck It" out loud and walked up to the front door. I knocked on Eric's door and waited. I didn't know what I'd say, but it was time to take some action. No one answered. I knocked again louder, still no movement from inside the house. Now I didn't know what to think. I went back to my truck but stood outside leaning on the hood. I decided to walk down to the Robinson house.

After several loud knocks, I knew that no one was there, either. What the hell was going on? I couldn't figure it out the whole way back to my truck. I had passed the red truck, but everything still looked the same. Maybe he was just scouting it out. Then, I saw something that wasn't right. A very nice Camaro was parked on the side of the street in front of Eric's house. Nobody who wants their car to be there in the morning would leave that car on the street. I had never seen it before, but it looked out of place. That could have been Eric's car. Maybe he grabbed them while they walked to it. No, that would be too risky. Maybe they never made it that far.

I decided to walk around the house and check if there was a back door. As I rounded the corner, I saw the newest crime scene. The window was broken, and duct tape held it together. As I inspected the window, I thought that it actually wasn't a half bad idea if you were going to break in. I looked around and entered the same window that Brian Walker must have entered.

My gun was pulled out, and I cleared the downstairs first. I didn't know whether to expect dead bodies or nothing at all. When I got to the upstairs bedroom, I peeked in but didn't see anyone. The room smelled like piss and sex. They must be into some weird shit around here. Then, I saw the actual piss stain on the bed and where it looked like a scuffle might have happened. They obviously weren't here, so if I had to guess, this was where he must have abducted them. My phone was in my hand, but I didn't open it.

I was in a real predicament now. If I called this in, they would wonder why in the hell I walked around the house and came in. Why was I even at this house to begin with? They might even start to think that I was in on it. My phone number called Brian's today, and now I mysteriously knew who was taken that night. This did not look good. I needed to get out of there before it got any worse. I couldn't crawl back out of the window. What if someone saw me now? Then I'd be the white guy they identified. I stood on the stairs trying to fit the pieces together. Finally, an idea came to me.

Chapter 15

Brian

The morning of June 9th

"Let me go you sick fucker!" Kendra yelled as I opened the last door. She hung from the ceiling with her hands above her head. Her feet weren't chained to the floor, and as I approached, she kicked at me. I stepped back and let her miss. The duct tape was still over her eyes, and she continued to kick wildly. I shook my head and walked toward Devon. I tossed him a bag with six donuts and an orange juice in it.

"How do you like your new roommates?" I asked.

"Is Terrance alive?" he responded.

I shrugged my shoulders. "That's up to him. I hope he is. I went through a lot of trouble just to have him die in less than a day. My guess is that he's alive."

The room was starting to stink. Devon's bathroom bucket didn't get dumped yesterday, and that wasn't a chore a person wanted to miss. Once I was done with Kendra and Eric, I'd have to get rid of it.

"Are you ready to take your blindfold off?" I asked.

"Fuck you! Where's Eric?" She yelled.

I looked toward the open door and saw Eric chained to the chair in the other room. Three was too many to have in one room. Besides, I was going to need some room to maneuver with him. Eric sat there watching us but didn't move. He didn't even look scared sitting there. Eric had more confidence than all of the others. He was chained to a chair, a few feet from where his friend Terrance was buried while his girlfriend hung from the ceiling in the other room, and still he had the confidence to not be afraid. My grandpa's favorite saying rang true, "Confidence: It's the food to the wise man but the liquor to the fool."

"Eric is fine. Do you want me to take off your blindfold or not?" I asked again.

"Yes, get this fucker off me," she said.

"If you kick me while I'm close, I promise it won't end well for you," I said.

I leaned forward and started to peel the duct tape from Kendra's head. It grasped onto hair, eyebrows, and whatever else was underneath it. She started to scream. I tried to steadily pull until she decided to kick me in the thigh. Then, I ripped off all the tape in one motion. It took off most of her left eyebrow, and she began crying. A little blood ran down her face.

"Eric's going to kill you!" She screamed.

I pointed to the other room, where she saw Eric chained to the chair with duct tape across his mouth. He was shirtless, and there was a little dried blood on his left shoulder from the pistol whipping last night.

"I doubt that," I said to her in a calm voice. Then I continued with, "Do you know why you're here? Did Devon get a chance to fill you in?"

Tears were streaming down her face, but it was not because of fear or being injured. Kendra was having a temper tantrum and began screaming incoherently. The same way a father would, I waited her out. Finally, she started to make sense again.

"Fuck you and your fucking bitch. I'm glad she's dead. She deserved everything she got," she said.

"What people deserve will be discussed shortly. But if I were you, I'd refrain from calling my dead wife names. That isn't going to improve your situation," I said.

She looked right at me, "She was a fucking cunt."

I stepped forward and backhand her with a closed fist. Her head whipped back. Blood ran down from her chin. I turned around and looked to the ceiling. I spoke to myself out loud. "I'm sorry, Hannah. You wouldn't have wanted me to hit a woman. But hopefully you'll understand this one time."

I turned back around. "Today you're going to learn that there are consequences for your actions. Part of me wants to just kill you, but that wouldn't be completing the circle. That would be taking my personal feelings into it. That wouldn't make me a good Christian, would it?"

Kendra stared at me, and for the first time, the fear was flickering in her eyes. She finally knew that today was going to be filled with pain, and there was nothing she could do about it.

"Do you read the Bible, Kendra? I asked.

"No," she said.

"A few times it talks about cutting off a person's hand to keep him from committing sin. I'm paraphrasing, but it basically says, "If your hand tempts you to commit sin, then cut it off." Your hands don't seem to be your problem. What is the part that keeps tempting you?" I asked.

Kendra shook her head that she didn't know. The fear was growing inside her.

"What did you do to get kicked out of school?" I asked.

She continued to be silent. Sweat began to run down her forehead. I was sure the walls were closing in on her right about now.

"Do you know, Devon?" I asked, but he didn't move or make a sound. "I do. I paid a high school counselor two hundred bucks to find out. She told me that during Kendra's sophomore year of high school, she attacked a little Asian girl in the cafeteria. She said Kendra knocked her down and stomped her head until she was restrained. When asked why she did it, the counselor said that Kendra said, 'Because the little bitch wore the same shirt as I did.' That's one heck of a reason to stomp someone's head isn't it?"

Kendra looked like fear had swallowed her now. She pleaded with me, "Please don't do this. Please."

"Do you remember what you did to my wife? You kicked her while she was on the ground. It seems like we've established what part of you tempts you the most," I said.

"Please don't cut my foot off. I didn't mean to," she said.

"You didn't mean to? Yes, you did. Our habits speak louder than our words," I said and cracked my knuckles. "But I'm not a doctor. If I cut your foot off, I'm quite sure you'd be dead very fast. That's not the point. So, we're going to plan B."

I pointed toward the ground at her feet. She looked down to see a vise bolted to the ground. This was the kind you would normally see on the table at a shop. You place an object inside the grip and turn the lever until it was tight. There was no stopping device, so you can tighten it as tight as you need to.

"Instead of cutting your foot off and having you bleed to death. I'm going to place your foot inside the vice and tighten it until, well, until your foot is as good as gone."

Kendra screamed at the top of her lungs, but this time, I grabbed her left foot and handcuffed it. I had a rope tied to the other end, and I tightened it. In the corner, there was a spare hook, so I tied the rope there. That way, when I placed her right foot in the vise, she couldn't kick me with her left foot. She struggled, but like a calf about to be branded, her fate was inevitable.

When I got a hold of her right foot, she screamed and did everything in her power to keep it out of the vise. I thought about the tranquilizer, but she needed to feel the pain. I began tightening the vise until her right foot could no longer wiggle its way free. I stepped back and looked at her.

"You are about to feel an immense amount of pain. I suggest you think about the fact that you're lucky enough to still be alive after this is done. Hannah didn't get that chance," I said.

"Fuck her," Kendra defiantly yelled.

"So be it," I said and dropped to one knee. I cranked the vise one full turn at a time. In less than two turns, I could hear the first bones break. By the third turn, blood was coming out of the compound fractures. Kendra didn't feel the fourth turn because she passed out. I gave it one last pull, but there was too much resistance to clamp them together. I quickly unrolled the vise before her urine got on my hand. I stood up and looked at the mangled foot. She wouldn't be kicking anybody else with that one. I looked over to the open door and saw Eric sitting still. It was now time for the grand finale.

Chapter 16

Detective Owens

The morning of June 9th

C op cars swarmed Eric Hayes' house. Red and blue lights lit up the street in the early morning light. Eddie pulled up with bags under his eyes and a handkerchief in his hand. I met him at his car.

"Hop in my truck. I need to fill you in," I said. "Don't touch anything, either."

As he got in the truck, I started, "This is going to be a lot to take in, but try to follow ok?"

"Is there a test after?" He asked humorlessly.

"Nope, just a really important decision," I said and continued, "The house that was broken into belongs to Eric Hayes and Kendra Turner. They are now missing. The house that made the call this morning about the red truck that led us to being here belongs to Terrance Robinson. He and his little brother, Devon, are now also missing. The door to their house was wide open this morning. Are we clear so far?"

"Yeah, everyone is missing," Eddie said.

What I left out was that I was the one who made the call from the Robinson's house this morning and left the door open so that we'd now have a reason to look for them. Somebody had to start the ball rolling.

"Correct. This is where it gets a little crazy. Do you remember the list I showed the captain last year?" I asked.

He shook his head, so I continued. "Last year, I showed the captain a list of people I thought were involved in the Walker case. There were five people on my list. I didn't put it together until this morning. Guess the five people's names that were on my list," I asked.

"I remember that day, but you never showed me the list. I have no idea," Eddie said.

I put one finger up and added to it as I said their names. "Jared Jackson, Eric Hayes, Kendra Turner, Terrance Robinson, and Devon Robinson."

Eddie's jaw dropped, "Are you kidding me? You have got to be shitting me, right?"

"I shit you not, Eddie. I called Gavin this morning to see if Brian Walker had any properties near Milwaukee. He said no. But his credit card gets swiped at two gas stations pretty often. One is in his home town of Omro, and the other is just north of Milwaukee," I said.

The dots were starting to connect for him. "Brian Walker, holy shit," he said.

"Exactly. I think that we need to head to Omro right now. He is our best suspect, and the clock is ticking," I said.

"How would he have found them, though? That doesn't add up," Eddie said.

"It's been two years. They all live on the same fricken street. If he stumbled on one, he'd run into the others. How do you think I found them?" I asked.

"That's true. What do you think we should do?" He asked.

"I think we grab Webb and Davis and drive straight there. If he has them, then we might save their lives. If it's not him, then at least we cross the biggest name off our list," I said.

"Should we call the captain and see what he thinks?" Eddie asked.

"Fuck him. If we're right, he'll be happy, and if we're wrong, he'll never know," I said. "This is a defining moment Eddie. What do you want to do?"

Eddie looked nervous, but to my surprise said, "Ok, let's do it."

I grabbed Webb and Davis, and we headed north. My black truck led the way. Eddie sniffled as we wove in and out of traffic on I-41. The clock kept ticking, and I knew there was a lot riding on this hunch.

Chapter 17

Brian

The morning of June 9th

"Can you see Eric from where you're at?" I asked Devon.

He looked up and through the door and nodded his head. By now, I thought Devon just wanted to live, so he played his part very well. I walked through the door and up to Eric. I leaned down and ripped the tape off his lips. He just nodded his head demonstratively.

"I saved you for last, Eric. Do you know why?" I asked.

"I have no idea who you are, and I don't give a shit. If I get out of this chair, I'm going to fuck you up for what you just did to Kendra. I promise you that," he said.

"You're not in a position to be making threats. I made sure that you got to watch what I did to Kendra because I had to watch what you did Hannah," I said.

"Who in the hell is Hannah? I don't even know any Hannahs," he said, confused.

Right then, I realized that he didn't spend the night in the room with Devon, so he probably didn't know what I was talking about. I walked over to the stone table and sat on it.

"Two years ago, my wife and I were attacked by you, Kendra, Terrance, and Jared. My little buddy over there drove the getaway car," I said as I pointed to the room with Devon. "Two days ago, I stabbed Jared one hundred times because he stabbed my wife once. Yesterday, I buried Terrance right there," I pointed at the shovel sticking out of the dirt. "I buried him alive, because he didn't do anything to her during the attack. You saw me mangle your girlfriend's foot because she kicked Hannah. Now, that brings me to you. The man that punched her in the face and pushed her into the cement that ended up killing her," I said.

"For you, I thought of so many sick things that I shouldn't even talk about. I was going to castrate you, blind you, hell, maybe try to skin you while you were still alive. But that didn't meet my theme. Those would have made me feel good, but they wouldn't have been true revenge. You wouldn't have felt what she felt."

Eric listened but didn't try to interrupt like Kendra had. He was either remembering that night or knew his fate was sealed by the look on my face.

"The hate that fills my heart for you cannot be expressed. You took the one person in the world that I loved more than myself. You took her from me, and I never got see her do anything that made me love her again. You cannot even start to comprehend what I feel. This bullshit you feel for Kendra is amateur. You love her now, but when something better would have come along, you would have split before the door could shut." I took a deep breath, "Instead, I got to watch Hannah lie in a hospital bed for over a week before she finally passed. Every day, I prayed to God to have her come back until one day, I quit believing. You even took my belief in God from me. Do you know what that's like?"

He didn't respond. He knew there was no answer at that point.

"No, you don't. Over the past year, I have started to regain my faith. Belief is something we all need to help justify what we do every day. It helped me justify what I did to all of you. So, my final scripture in this mink building is the most classic of them all. An eye for an eye, Eric," I said and lifted the baseball bat that was sitting on the table.

"You punched Hannah and then cracked her head open. You didn't know whether she'd live or die. So, your fate will be the same. I'm going to pop you in the mouth with the end of this bat, to count as a punch. Then, I'm going to stand behind you and take the biggest swing I possibly can at the back of your head. Whether you live or die from that moment doesn't matter. The circle will be complete."

Eric never said a word. He stared me down like I was one of the punks on Roosevelt Street that feared him. He started to speak, but I stopped him. I jabbed the bat directly into his mouth. Blood immediately started flowing, and when his head came back up, I could see three teeth missing. Through his pain, he smiled at me and said, "This ain't gonna bring her back."

I stepped around the back of Eric and held the bat like a baseball player. I thought of Hannah lying in the hospital bed and the day we laid her in the grave. Two years of pure hate helped me swing the bat as hard as I possibly could. I stepped into the swing and felt the clunk as the bat connected with his head. There was a vibration in my hands. Eric's head went forward and shot backwards before coming back forward to rest. He didn't move. Blood began pouring out of his mouth and a little out of his ears.

I dropped the bat and wiped the tears away from my eyes. A sense of accomplish warmed my body. I sat on the stone table and looked at the carnage in the mink building. My business was done here, but that didn't mean my circle was complete yet. There were others who had betrayed Hannah's memory, and they had to be brought to light so that it didn't happen to others in the future.

"Time to go, Devon. We've done all we can do in here," I said.

"Where are we going? We can't leave Terrance," Devon said.

"If I had to guess, my friend Detective Owens, will find him soon enough. My bet is that he'll be here tonight, but we better take the back roads just in case. We've got time; our host doesn't even know we're coming tonight," I said.

Chapter 18

Detective Owens

The morning of June 9th

We pulled into Brian Walker's driveway and sped to his house. His little farm looked empty. There weren't any cows in the fields surrounding the house. There was an old green tractor broken down by the barn. The blue dually sat in the front of the house. I parked behind it, in case he tried to run, and continued to scan the property. I didn't see any animals anywhere. The worst part was that I didn't see the old red truck.

Eddie pulled his weapon like we were on an episode of Cops. Webb and Davis followed suit, so I figured what the hell and pulled my pistol too. We approached the house. Webb and Davis took the back while Eddie and I walked to the front door.

"I'll take the lead," I said to Eddie.

He nodded and coughed into his shoulder. I knocked on the front door. The big window next to the door gave me a perfect view of the living room. With one look, I could tell there was no one in the house. It looked like he hadn't been home for awhile.

"Sorry, Eddie," I said as I kicked in the front door.

"Jesus Christ, Jack," Eddie said.

"I'm not turning back now," I said.

We began to clear the house. I went into the living room, but there were only a few pictures of Hannah and Brian. Everything looked like it had been perfectly cleaned about two weeks ago. I took my finger and wiped the top of the television. There was a very light coat of dust.

"The kitchen is clear," Eddie yelled.

We made our way down the hall and cleared the three bedrooms. Just as I expected, he wasn't here. Brian had made a point to clean this place and keep it clean. Everything was in perfect order until I walked into the master bathroom. There was a dirty pair of pants in the hamper. I lifted them up and saw that blood had splattered on the right knee. The hunch was correct. He must have brought them back here to his house.

"Check the basement, Webb. Make sure no one is down there," I yelled as they entered. "We need to check the barn. If blood splattered on his pants, then they could have been out there," I said to Eddie.

We walked out to the cow barn but there was one big problem: there weren't any cows. It still smelled like cow shit, but there weren't any cows anywhere. First, we cleared the grain room. There was grain in a few bins, but other than an old rope on the wall, the room was empty. Then, we cleared the medicine room. It was also empty. There was an old fridge in the corner, so I went and opened it. Not one bottle of medicine to be found. I slammed the door.

"This isn't right, Eddie. Who the fuck raises cattle but doesn't have any cattle? No feed, no medicine, no dog, none of this is right," I said.

Eddie contemplated and then spoke, "Maybe he went broke and had to sell everything."

"That could be. Or maybe he knew the end was near and sold them all. He might as well cash out while he's still alive. It would have let him devote all of his time to this task," I said. "But where in the hell did he do it?"

As we walked outside, Webb and Davis met us. They couldn't hide their confusion.

"Nothing in the basement, not a sign anyone has been in there for awhile," Davis said.

We stood outside until I finally saw the truck tracks leading past the barn and towards the east. I followed them with my eyes until I saw a little brick building by the tree line. I focused to make sure my eyes weren't fooling me.

"Right there, on the tree line. Do you guys see it?" I asked.

All three of them squinted and nodded in unison. As we neared the building, we all knew it was the place. Fresh tire tracks led to the front door. The building looked ancient; paint was nonexistent on the bricks. There was a line in the sand that showed where the door had recently opened. The door handle stuck a little, and I had to jerk the door to swing it towards us.

We stepped through the door, and the smell of animal shit surrounded us. They must have housed animals in here years ago. We continued to the second door, and it slid open easily. The scene I had expected to see at the house was now in front of me. Eric Hayes was chained to a chair in the middle of the floor. His head was split open and blood pooled in his lap. The guilty Louisville slugger rested in some of his blood on the floor.

The corner of the room was covered with sand, and a shovel rested on top. There were pipes coming up to the surface. I didn't know if that was part of his sick game or just a fixture in this old building. The other door in the room was open, and as I approached it, I nearly jumped out of my skin when I heard a woman's voice call out, "Is somebody there? HELP!"

I rushed to the door to find Kendra Turner hanging from the ceiling. She hung there with her right foot off the ground. It looked like it had been run over by a tractor. The skin was open, and I could see bone sticking out. Kendra began crying uncontrollably when I entered the room. She probably had never been happier to a see a cop in her life.

I walked up to her and then followed the chain to the corner of the room to let her down. Eddie held her in his arms so she didn't have to put weight on her foot. She clutched him like a five year old who didn't want to go to school.

"Kendra, where is Brian Walker?" I asked.

"I don't know. He took Devon and left. Is Eric dead?" She asked through the tears.

"Devon Robinson is with him?"

She nodded but didn't speak. She was getting a good look at what used to be her foot. She flung her head back and wailed.

"Was there anyone else here?" I asked.

"Devon was here the whole time," she pointed at the mattress in the corner. "The sick bastard made him watch what he did to us. He killed Jared and then T. Oh my God, T. He's in the other room."

"Only Eric was in the room," Eddie said. "Did he take him too?"

"No, he's buried in there. He's alive. He buried him alive. You have to see if he's still alive!" She exclaimed.

I ran into the other room and grabbed the shovel. I dug as fast I could until I heard a clunk. There was something buried under the sand. That was when it hit me; the pipes coming up were for air. It took longer than I would have liked, but we finally uncovered the coffin. There was a lock on the side. I hit it repeatedly with the shovel until Officer Davis handed me a key. "This was hanging on the second door handle."

The lock came off, and we lifted the lid. Terrance shielded his face with both hands. Once I grabbed his hand, I realized he wasn't shielding himself from the light; it was the fear of whoever opened the coffin. His eyes were opened wide, and he was in shock. There was no use trying to get any information from him. He wouldn't be able to talk for awhile, if ever. Terrance Robinson would forever be a PTSD case on steroids.

I went back to Kendra and tried to get answers. "Did he say where they were going? Anything you can remember would help us."

"He never said where they were going. He did this because we attacked his wife years ago," she said.

"Did you guys attack them that night?" Eddie asked.

She nodded her head and said, "We never meant to kill her. We were just going to rough them up. I didn't even know she died until now."

Eddie and I left Kendra with Officer Davis and stepped outside. The sun felt good after digging that coffin out.

"Looks like you were right," Eddie said.

"Yeah, kind of wish I wasn't now," I said.

"What do we do now? He's still out there," Eddie said.

"I can't believe I'm about to say this, but you better call the captain. The crime scene is shit now, but we need to get the unit out here. At least we have two witnesses, well, one and a half. As for Brian, I don't know what his next move is, but we need to find him before he kills Devon Robinson," I said.

"I wonder why he didn't just kill him in there?" Eddie asked.

"I don't know, but I bet we're going to find out," I said.

Chapter 19

Brian

The night of June 9th

After a quick pit stop to drop something off, Devon and I pulled into River Hills, a nice neighborhood just outside of Milwaukee. It wasn't where the elite lived, but it was only one notch below. It was mostly older families where every lawn was mowed perfectly. We continued up Hope Road, that's the real name of the street, until we saw number 5465. The mailbox was black and had one name on it: Stroup.

My headlights turned off as I turned into his driveway. Devon was handcuffed and gagged in the backseat. I stepped out of the truck and walked up the door. The neighborhood reminded me of Pleasantville. I didn't wear a mask or dress in black. If the neighbors looked over, I didn't want them to be suspicious of anything. The outside light flipped on before I had a chance to pull my hands out of my pockets. The door swung open, and a bald man stood in front of me in a white t-shirt and slacks.

I smiled and looked him in the eyes, "Captain Stroup?"

"Yes sir, what can I do for you?" He said.

I pulled the small can of mace from my pocket and sprayed him directly in the eyes. I bought it three months ago from a woman named

Elizabeth Stuart on craigslist. The stream hit him directly in the left eye before he tried to cover his face. I continued spraying until he turned his back and stumbled into his house. At that point, I dropped the mace and pulled out my pistol. I whipped him in the back of the head, but he only dropped to one knee. Then I kicked him in the back of head with my heel, but to my surprise, the captain still didn't go down. He was wiping his eyes with both hands. I knew this next blow better put him out, or I might have a real fight on my hands. I took my pistol and hit him in the back of the head hard enough that he went completely down to the floor.

The blinds fluttered as the door slammed. I ran through the hallway to the dining room. I grabbed the first chair and brought it back into the front room. The Captain was a fat man, but I managed to get him into the chair. I felt like a Nascar pit crew member as I duct taped both wrists and his ankles to the chair. I made sure the duct tape covered his wrists, not his hands. As I finished his last ankle, the Captain tried speaking.

"Who in the hell are you?" He slurred.

I stretched a piece of duct tape across his bobbing head and then said, "You'll find out soon enough."

Before I opened the door, I took a deep breath to compose myself. I strolled to the backseat of my red truck and opened Devon's door. He sat completely calm like he was waiting for me to come out of the bank.

"Lean over while I uncuff you," I said.

He did what I asked and didn't put up a fight. In the matter of a few days, Devon had submitted. Sometimes, horses take weeks to submit, but Devon broke in a couple days. The will to live was stronger than his will to fight. If any neighbors would have looked over, they would have thought Devon and I walked into Captain Stroup's home with our arms linked. What they would have seen if they looked closer was that my other hand held a .38 to his ribs. Even a broke horse will buck if they think they can get away with it.

Once Devon was handcuffed to another chair, I looked around until I found the Captain's cell phone. It was sitting on the table by his unfinished tuna sandwich. I brought the phone and two chairs back into the front room. I set the first chair directly in front of the Captain with the phone perched on top.

"No passcode, Captain? You need to get with the times," I said as I pulled up his camera. I leaned forward and pulled the duct tape off his mouth.

"Do you know who I am? I'm a captain on the fucking police force!" He shouted.

"I know exactly who you are," I said.

"What do you want? Is this some kind of ransom?" He asked.

"No, no ransom. I'm more interested in answers than I am money," I said.

"Answers to what?" He asked.

I turned his video camera on and made sure it was pointing at him. I sat down in the second chair and began, "Let me tell you how this is going to work. We are going to have a little interview, and everyone is going to see it. When we're done, I'm going to post it to your Facebook, YouTube, and send it to every one of your contacts. I'm guessing you have some powerful friends in there," I said and leaned toward him.

"There is one catch though," I said and pulled out a pair of garden pruners from my pocket. "It's very important that you tell the truth. If I think you're lying to me, I'm going to cut off one of your fingers."

"You crazy, son of a bitch; this will never hold up," he spluttered.

"You're right, it will never hold up in court. But in today's world, courts don't really matter. You're going to be tried in the court of public opinion. Within an hour of us finishing, the whole world will know what you did," I said.

"You're Brian Walker aren't you? They found your little murder compound today, you sick bastard. You better care what the courts think because they're going to fry your ass," he said.

I took a deep breath and spoke into the camera, "Two years ago, Lamar Webb was shot by a cop, and in the days following, Milwaukee had several nights of rioting. The Black Lives Matter movement swept the city and flooded the news. On June 5th, my wife, Hannah, and I were attacked at a Kwik Stop. The people who attacked us were mostly black. None of them were ever arrested, and I believe it was because of their color. It was the one time where arresting black people looked bad. And because of that, my wife, who died because of the attack, was denied justice," I said and looked back at the Captain.

"Why was no one ever arrested?" I asked.

"We did everything we could to find your attackers," the captain said.

"Are you left or right handed?" I asked.

The captain looked confused, "I'm right handed," he answered.

"The next time you lie to me, I'm going to cut off your right index finger. Tell me the truth. Why was no one ever arrested?"

"I'm telling you the truth," he started, and I unclipped the pruners' lock. "Ok, you want details. From what I remember, there was a witness, but she wasn't credible."

"What do you mean, not credible?" I asked

"Her story had holes in it. She didn't know what she saw," he said.

"What about me? Was I not credible?" I asked.

"You were knocked out. Your descriptions were too vague," he said.

"Fair enough. In Cleveland, cops got in trouble for not arresting black people during the riots. Did that happen here?" I asked.

"Absolutely not. I would never do that," he said and looked at the phone.

I watched his head turn a different shade of red, and I knew he was lying. Caption Stroup needed to learn how serious I was at finding the truth. I stepped out of my chair and grabbed his right hand before he could make a fist. His chair tipped back, but I didn't let it fall.

"You did this," I said and placed the pruners' blades on each side of his index finger. Once the clipper was drawing blood, I used both hands to cut off his finger. It took two seconds of pushing, but the blades came together. It wasn't any harder than cutting a small branch.

"Fuck!" the Captain yelled. "Fuck you, you piece of shit."

"Go ahead; get it out of your system," I said. I wrapped duct tape around his bloody nub. It wouldn't stop the bleeding, but it was tight enough that he wouldn't bleed to death.

"Now, tell me the truth. Is that what happened here?" I asked.

The captain scrunched his face. His head was the color of rage. I sat back down and waited for his answer.

"Ok. Yes. Yes, that is what happened here," he said. "Are you happy?"

"I don't want you to tell me what I want to hear. I want you to tell me the truth. I don't care what it is; I just want the whole truth," I said.

"We couldn't afford to have the riots continue to escalate. The city was on fire, and it was ready to explode. If we would have arrested a group of black people at that time, the whole thing could have blown up. With the city already burning, one person wasn't worth lighting the rest of it," he said.

I leaned back in my chair and soaked up the truth. For years, I thought that was what happened, but it was different to actually hear him say it was true. I felt like a parent who was disappointed by their kid's poor decision. The police department chose politics over justice, and Hannah was the one that suffered the most because of it.

"And the truth shall set you free," I said. "Detective Thompson and Detective Owens were on the case. Do you think they did their best to find our attackers?"

The captain nodded adamantly and said, "They did nothing wrong. They followed my direction to a T. I know that Owens continued to look long after the case was over. Don't go after them. The buck stops with me," he said.

My chair tipped over as I stood up. I crouched in front of the captain and patted him on the leg. "You didn't raise a finger to help Hannah, now you don't have a finger. Next time you look at your right hand, you'll know to do the right thing," I said.

The Captain's eyes started to tear up. His head was about to explode from anger, but I had struck a nerve. The thought of being a

238

good cop stirred deep within most policemen even if they'd strayed. They would not have chosen that career if it wasn't in their soul.

I turned around and faced the camera phone. This small device was about to deliver my message to the world. I needed to make sure it delivered the one I needed it to.

"I have one final message. It has already been delivered, and when you watch this, you'll know who you are. By the end of tonight, my goal is that you'll see my message clearly. When it's over, I'll simply fly away like a sparrow to the place where it all began," I said.

Chapter 20

Detective Owens

The night of June 9th

ddie and I were just outside the city when our phones dinged at the same time. We both had a message from the captain. "What is it?" I asked.

"A video. It's probably just a funny one," Eddie said and opened the link.

As the video started, Eddie gasped. When he finally composed himself, he looked at me and said, "He's got the captain."

We were nearing Eddie's house, so I sped up. I pulled over in front of his house, and he restarted the video. Neither one of us spoke. We watched our captain get his finger cut off by Brian Walker, and I nearly threw up. The captain is a son of a bitch, but that was too far. He was the captain of the damn police force, not an everyday criminal.

When Brian finished speaking, the video cut out. I felt like the walls of the truck were shrinking in on me. The last part of his message had been directed at me. The sparrow reference was his little way of calling me out. But for what? Does he want me to see his message clearly? Or was that part for Eddie? He said he had delivered his message already? I had so many questions and very few answers.

"Jack, I am legitimately scared," Eddie said, and his look matched his statement. "There is no doubt in my mind that he's coming after me next. Everyone that fucked this guy over has gotten it except me. I can't stay at my house tonight."

"We're staying together tonight. I don't know if it's you or me that he's after, but he's going to have to take us both if he wants either one of us," I said.

"Why would he want you? You're the one who tried to solve his case. I'm the one who blindly followed the Captain two years ago. I'm fucked, man. I'm telling you: he's coming after me," he said.

Eddie had a point, but it was the wrong time to finally give him credit. As things settled in my mind, I began to think that Eddie was his next target. During our conversation a year ago, I remember the two of them coming up. I needed to keep Eddie alive tonight, and hopefully, that would allow enough time for someone to find Brian Walker.

We sat in the truck, re-watching the end of the video. Eddie slid his finger back and forth along his iPhone, trying to find the meaning of the message.

"So, he says that the message has been delivered. Do you know what he's talking about?" He asked.

"Not yet. Maybe he meant that his message of revenge was delivered, but I don't know. What do you think?" I asked.

"No fucking idea," Eddie responded. "You'll know who you are. That part's easy: me. 'By the end of tonight, I hope you'll see my message clearly.' I'm not seeing shit clearly right now," Eddie said and wiped his eyes.

"I think he means that we'll understand why he did it, but I don't know. Maybe it's something completely different," I said.

Eddie began coughing uncontrollably. His body looked like it was convulsing for thirty seconds. When he finally gave himself a moment to breathe, he wiped away the tears that had formed. He was tip toeing the line between crying because of the situation and tearing up from being sick. I let him off the hook either way.

"This is ridiculous, man. I need to go get my medicine. I need some Nyquil and my eye drops," Eddie said.

There were times during that day when Eddie looked fine, and then there were times, like right now, where he looked like death was knocking on his door. We were sitting in front of his house, and it seemed stupid to not let him go get his medicine.

"I better go with you," I said.

"Dude, it's going to take two minutes. If I'm not back in two minutes, come in guns blazing," he said, and the dome light came on as his door opened.

"Pull your weapon," I said. "I'm serious. If you walk in there, walk in with it drawn."

Eddie pulled it out and held it up for inspection. Sarcastically he said, "Good enough for you?"

"Are you sure you don't want me to go with you?" I asked one last time.

"I'm not a little kid. Two minutes," he said and crossed the street.

Eddie might not be a twelve year old, but I watched the clock like a single mom approaching midnight. The seconds felt like minutes, and I caught myself holding my breath. My collar tightened around my neck, and finally I said, "To hell with this" and stepped out of the truck. I was almost to Eddie's front door when it opened. I pulled my weapon, and we were in a Mexican standoff with guns drawn. Eddie and I took a collective sigh as our guns lowered.

"Jesus Christ man, you scared the shit out of me," Eddie said.

"I thought you were… well, fuck it, let's go back to the truck," I said

Eddie had a Wal-Mart bag with two items: a half empty bottle of Nyquil and small bottle of ClearEyes. He poured himself two capfuls of Nyquil and winced like he just took a shot of tequila after each one.

"What message do you think he already delivered to you? I think it had to have been when he killed Jared Jackson. He laid him in your driveway," I said.

"That's true. He stabbed in one hundred times for stabbing his wife once. What's that mean he's going to do to me?" He asked.

"I don't know. Was there anything else on his body?" I asked.

Eddie paused, "I don't think so, nothing that I can remember," Eddie pulled out the small bottle of ClearEyes. "I can't believe I forgot this today, I left it right on the counter."

I kept replaying the scene with Jared Jackson in my head. I could see the stab wounds and the placement of the body. I don't think that was his message. Eddie sniffled and opened the bottle of ClearEyes. I had the faintest wiff of the solution and I thought back to Jared's house. The house was a wreck, but there was one thing out of place. The message on the mirror: *A blind eye for a blind eye.* I looked over to Eddie's head which was now tipped back and knew I recognized the smell.

"No," I yelled, but it was too late. Eddie had squirted bleach directly into his eye. He dropped the bottle and began rubbing his eye vigorously. He bobbed back and forth in the seat.

"My eye, my eye!" He screamed. "It's on fire! Help me!"

There wasn't a water bottle in my truck, so I got out and ran to the other side of the truck to open Eddie's door. I held his arm as we sprinted into the house. Eddie put his head under the kitchen faucet and let the water run over his eye. I pulled out my cell phone and called an ambulance.

"It burns man," Eddie cried over and over.

"It's going to be all right. Just let the water run over it. The ambulance is on its way," I said.

The ambulance lights came and left with Eddie. I stayed behind this time. My truck's doors were still open when I got back to it. I shut the passenger door and stopped to think what had happened. Brian Walker had struck again. The clever bastard had planted that message days ago in Jared Jackson's house and then told us it was coming tonight. "My goal is that you'll see my message clearly" he had said. As clear as ClearEyes filled with bleach will let you.

My phone started to ring, and I looked at the clock. It was almost two in the morning. Maybe they caught the son of a bitch sleeping at a rest area. When I looked at my phone, I nearly dropped it. It said *Unknown,* but I knew whose number was calling.

Chapter 21

Brian

The morning of June 10th

Detective Owens answered on the first ring. The phone was filled with silence. Both of us breathed into the phone, but neither wanted to be the first to speak. Sometimes hunters are so busy looking at the tracks that they forget to look up and see the mountain lion. I wasn't in a tree, but I had watched Detective Owens and Detective Thompson all night.

"Judging by the ambulance leaving, I'm guessing that Eddie got my message," I said.

"Yeah, he got your message loud and clear," Owens said. "When you're in prison, you'll have to tell me how you pulled that off."

"I might as well tell you right now because there will be no prison for me. Besides, you should know, you helped me," I said.

"Bullshit, I helped you. Everything you've done is on your head, not mine," Owens said.

"I take full responsibility for it all, but you did help. I had something else planned for Eddie's eye, but you were the one who told me he was sick. Do you remember that? 'Just a runny nose and watery eyes' you said. Don't feel bad though. Either way, he had it coming. He turned a blind eye to Hannah's case, and now he has a blind eye," I said.

245

I tapped my blinker and turned onto another street. I waited to see the ambulance leave, but there was no need to push the envelope and have Detective Owens find me tonight, especially when we were this close to the end.

"You're the smartest dumb country boy that I've ever met, but your run is coming to an end. I'll find you, and I'm going to do it damn quick," he said.

"I know you are, Detective Owens. Didn't you listen to the last part of my message? It was for you," I said.

There was a pause on the line. He must have been connecting the dots. "Fly away like a sparrow to the place where it began," he finally replied. "So, you're going back to the Kwik Stop?"

"No, we are going back to the Kwik Stop. You are going to meet me there tomorrow at eight in the morning," I said.

"You're turning yourself in?" He asked.

"You'll find out. There are some rules though. You are allowed to bring one other police officer with you. I'm assuming Eddie won't be available. If there are any more, I will kill Devon on the spot. If you are more than five minutes early, I will kill Devon. If you are five minutes late, guess what I'm going to do?" I asked.

"I get it. You'll kill Devon," he said.

"Correct. Tomorrow will go very smoothly if you follow these rules," I said.

"I wish you'd tell me what your plan is to not go to prison. I don't see a road for you that doesn't end there," he said.

I laughed and said, "Detective Owens, you're going to get your wish tomorrow. Don't be late, and follow the rules." I clicked off my cell phone and removed the battery. I threw it out the window. The table was set to complete the final circle.

Chapter 22

Detective Owens

The morning of June 10th

Officer Davis and I sat a quarter mile from the Kwik Stop waiting for the clock to strike eight. I picked him up at seven o'clock, and we'd been waiting for thirty minutes in that same spot. The odds of Brian Walker killing Devon because we were late were probably slim, but I wasn't going to risk his life on my hunch. He said that if I followed the rules, it would go smoothly. Brian might be a murderer, but so far, he had been a man of his word.

I chose Officer Davis because he was an older, dependable cop. I trusted him more than anyone on the force, and I knew that if this whole thing went south, he'd be willing to pull the trigger. The clock turned to 7:59, and I looked at him.

"All right, one last time, just like we talked about. When we get there, you back me up. Don't make a move until I do. Make sure you have your weapon on him, but don't shoot unless you are sure that he is going to shoot either me or Devon. Do you understand?" I asked.

Officer Davis nodded his head while keeping eye contact and finally asked, "Where do you want me positioned?"

"It's tricky until we see where he is, but I'd position so that you have a clear shot. Make sure you don't flank him, though. I don't want him getting nervous and doing something stupid. I also don't want you to be right beside me. Most likely, if he's going to fire at someone, it's going to be me. You don't need to catch a stray bullet," I said

"I'm not afraid to stand beside you," he said and paused. "I know what I signed up for."

"I know; that's why I picked you. But it's still the same: keep your ass away from me this morning," I said and gave him a nod.

The clock rolled to eight, and it was time to go. As we pulled in, I put my blinker on and saw the old red Ford. It was parked at the same diesel pump where the attack happened. Thank God the Kwik Stop wasn't too busy. I counted six cars in the parking lot, most of which were by the front doors. There was only one other car getting fuel, and he was a full lane away from Brian's truck.

My black Dodge came to a stop at the air compressor. Brian and I made eye contact and the son of bitch smiled at me. His door opened, and he and Devon stepped out. Devon appeared to be uninjured, but he did have his hands restrained and duct tape over his mouth. The next thing I saw was Brian Walker's pistol in his right hand. My gut started to tighten.

Officer Davis and I stepped out of the truck. I pointed to the side so that Brian could see him position himself away from me. I wanted him to know that he would never get both us at once. I was about twenty five feet from Brian, and Officer Davis was about thirty feet from me. We had created a little death triangle.

Brian spoke up. "Ok, that's far enough. That goes for your comrade as well."

I raised my side arm up and pointed it at Brian. Devon was restrained in front of Brian. He raised his gun up to Devon's head.

"Put the gun down, Brian, so we can talk. No need for anyone to get hurt today," I said levelly.

"I think we can talk just like this. I won't shoot unless you make me," Brian said.

This wasn't the ideal position for me to be in. Neither one of us could take the shot because Devon was a human shield for Brian. Yet I was standing in the open with no cover. I don't know if I was stupid or if I just knew that Brian probably didn't intend to kill me.

"Let's talk then. I'm not going to ask why you did it; I already know that answer. What's your end game here? How do you think you're not going to go to prison for things that you did?" I asked.

"Detective Owens, do you really know why I did it?" He asked.

"I do. You wanted revenge for Hannah. You did things to all of them that they had done to her," I said.

Brian laughed, "I did complete the circle of revenge on them, but you said that you knew why I did it. Try again."

I was confused. He did it because he wanted revenge for what they did to Hannah. I glanced at Officer Davis and he seemed steady so far.

"I guess, I don't know," I said

Brian shook his head, "You're a good detective. Someday, I hope you figure it out."

"Maybe I will, but how exactly do you think you're not going to prison for all of this?" I asked again.

"We're going to help each other out with that one. I'm going to grant you your wish," he said.

"Which wish are you talking about then?" I asked. "My wish right now is that you'd lay down your weapon and let Devon go."

There was starting to be people congregating by the door of the Kwik Stop. I could feel them watching as much as I could see them.

"Last year, you told me that once in your career, you'd like to stand in front of the bad guy and know that you were the good guy and shoot them like Wyatt Earp. Do you remember that?" He asked.

"Vaguely," I said

"Well, Devon and I are here to grant you that wish," he said.

I looked at him and thought he couldn't be serious. Devon's eyes were big and filling with tears. I could tell he wanted to run.

"Sorry to spoil your plan, but I'm not going to kill the kid. I don't operate like that," I said.

"That's why I'm not talking about the kid," Brian Walker kept his gun pointed at Devon's head but took one big step away from him. "I'm the bad man in this scenario. I kidnapped five people, killed two of them, and cut the police Captain's finger off. I'd say that makes me a bad guy. I didn't come here to surrender; I came here to be with Hannah. The only thing that I ask is that you make sure I go to see her."

This man was asking me to kill him. He was giving himself up but in a different way. The amazing part was that he didn't seem nervous or scared. He was the only one calm in our little triangle.

"I don't think I can do that," I said.

"Sure you can. That's why I brought Devon. He's my insurance policy. I knew that you'd never kill me without a reason. So, I'm going to give you one. If you don't kill me by the count of three, I'm going to

251

kill Devon." He looked at Devon, but I could still hear what he said to him. "I told you it was more likely that you'd be the death of me."

He cocked the hammer of his pistol, and I did the same. "Don't do this, Brian," I said.

"I know you'll miss me when I'm gone, but don't worry Jack. I have a napkin in my pocket that you can wipe your tears on afterward," he said.

Brian opened his chest completely up to me. He still held the gun to Devon's head, but he was looking at me.

"I can almost see the green pastures right now," he said and smiled. He looked like an old dog who was about to be put down and didn't hold it against his master for doing it.

"One... Two..." But before he could get to the number three, I fired my gun three times into the left section of his chest. Brian Walker fell backwards and released his gun. Devon ran to me with tears flowing down his face. I gave him a one armed hug and pointed to my truck. I walked up to Brian, but he was already crossing to the other side. I looked at Officer Davis, and he gave me an accepting nod.

He knelt down to pick up Brian's gun. I knelt down and pulled a napkin out of his front pocket. Officer Davis was inspecting the gun, so I shoved the napkin into my own. Officer Davis was shaking his head as he walked back over to me.

"What's up?" I asked.

"You aren't going to believe this, but there aren't any bullets in this gun," he said and showed me the empty chambers.

"He knew I wouldn't shoot him if I didn't think he was going to kill Devon. I guess all of his circles are complete now," I said.

Chapter 23

Detective Owens

The night of June 10th

The flames rose from the fire pit in my backyard. I stood alone reflecting on the day. This morning, I fired my weapon for the first time while on duty. Most have to fire it in some pointless manner or never do it at all. I had to take the life of someone that wanted to die. I was showered with praise at the station, but it had really been a mercy killing. Brian Walker wanted nothing more than to be with Hannah, and I allowed him to pass through the veil. I could have fired at his leg or just shot once, but I knew what I was doing. I put three bullets in his heart. I ended his life because deep down, I knew it was the right thing to do.

The very people who shot looks at me for sticking up for Brian two years ago were the ones who slapped me on the back today. They would all buy me beers at some point because I was the man who avenged the police force. Captain Stroup apologized to me on the phone. The most amazing part was that he meant it. Eddie cried in his hospital bed and hugged me like a brother. I'll probably get a promotion, and my career will be back on track. The man that derailed it ended up being the man who saved it. As Brian would say, another circle was complete.

The heat from the fire warmed my leg, and I took a step back. I put my hand in my pocket and felt the napkin. It had been in my pocket all day, and yet I never opened it. The truth was that I remembered writing the note to Brian, but I couldn't remember what it said. I unfolded it, and held it in the light of fire to read it.

Wishes come true on Roosevelt Street

She didn't deserve this!

Those ten words had changed the course of so many lives. Brian and I talked about wishes that day, and it seemed fitting. I had written those words to try and show that there was hope. I knew where the attackers were, and I wouldn't stop trying to catch them. I never could have known that he would turn into a vigilante and turn the whole city on its head. Or did I? Was I lying to myself?

Maybe, deep down, I had hoped that all of this would happen. Hannah Walker deserved justice, and we weren't giving it to her. I had tried and failed multiple times. Maybe, in my subconscious, I knew that he would do what I couldn't. Right now, the lines were blurred to the point that I would never know.

The backdoor swung open, and Jennifer stepped out. She had on a pair of shorts and a light sweatshirt. She looked beautiful in the glowing light. I looked back down at the note and read it again. "She didn't deserve this!" had been underlined. Brian had said those words to me in the hospital, and I could still feel the pain that filled them.

At that moment, it hit me. Brian had said that he hoped someday I'd figure out why he did it. I looked at Jennifer walking toward me and

254

understood. The things that he did were sickening and the most vengeful things that I had ever seen. But the reason he had done them was simple: love. He loved Hannah to the point that her revenge was the only thing that kept him alive, and when it was done, he left this world. For his sake, I hoped she was waiting for him in the green pasture today.

"How's my hero?" Jennifer asked.

I put my arm around her, and with my free hand threw the napkin in the fire. I watched as the paper shriveled and its smoke faded into the night sky. I looked into her beautiful eyes and saw my future. She was everything that I wanted. I smiled and said, "I'm no hero, but I do love you." I lightly kissed her on the lips and savored that kiss more than any before it.

Made in the USA
San Bernardino, CA
29 March 2020

66538467R00161